Winter Escapes

Around the world in four romances!

Pack your bags and leave the postfestivity blues behind! This January, Harlequin Romance presents a whirlwind tour to some stunning international locations—and we want you to join us. Whether you're looking for sun, sea or snow, we've got you covered. So let yourself be swept away by these beautiful romances and discover how four couples make it to their true destination... happy-ever-after!

Get ready for the trip of a lifetime with...

Their Hawaiian Marriage Reunion
by Cara Colter

Copenhagen Escape with the Billionaire
by Sophie Pembroke

Prince's Proposal for the Canadian Cameras
by Nina Singh

Cinderella's Moroccan Midnight Kiss
by Nina Milne

All available now!

T0284585

THEIR HAWAIIAN MARRIAGE REUNION

CARA COLTER

Harlequin
ROMANCE

If you purchased this book without a cover you should be aware that this book is stolen property. It was reported as "unsold and destroyed" to the publisher, and neither the author nor the publisher has received any payment for this "stripped book."

Harlequin® ROMANCE

Recycling programs for this product may not exist in your area.

ISBN-13: 978-1-335-21625-0

Their Hawaiian Marriage Reunion

Copyright © 2025 by Cara Colter

All rights reserved. No part of this book may be used or reproduced in any manner whatsoever without written permission.

Without limiting the author's and publisher's exclusive rights, any unauthorized use of this publication to train generative artificial intelligence (AI) technologies is expressly prohibited.

This is a work of fiction. Names, characters, places and incidents are either the product of the author's imagination or are used fictitiously. Any resemblance to actual persons, living or dead, businesses, companies, events or locales is entirely coincidental.

For questions and comments about the quality of this book, please contact us at CustomerService@Harlequin.com.

TM and ® are trademarks of Harlequin Enterprises ULC.

Harlequin Enterprises ULC
22 Adelaide St. West, 41st Floor
Toronto, Ontario M5H 4E3, Canada
www.Harlequin.com

Printed in U.S.A.

Cara Colter shares her home in beautiful British Columbia, Canada, with her husband of more than thirty years, an ancient crabby cat and several horses. She has three grown children and two grandsons.

Books by Cara Colter

Harlequin Romance

A White Christmas in Whistler

The Billionaire's Festive Reunion

Blossom and Bliss Weddings

Second Chance Hawaiian Honeymoon
Hawaiian Nights with the Best Man

Matchmaker and the Manhattan Millionaire
His Cinderella Next Door
The Wedding Planner's Christmas Wish
Snowbound with the Prince
Bahamas Escape with the Best Man
Snowed In with the Billionaire
Winning Over the Brooding Billionaire
Accidentally Engaged to the Billionaire

Visit the Author Profile page
at Harlequin.com for more titles.

Praise for
Cara Colter

"Ms. Colter's writing style is one you will
want to continue to read. Her descriptions
place you there.... This story does have a HEA but
leaves you wanting more."

—*Harlequin Junkie* on *His Convenient Royal Bride*

CHAPTER ONE

KAUAI.

Finally.

The Garden Isle was said to be one of the most beautiful places on the planet. And at any other time, Megan Hart, with her artist's eye and soul, would have taken in all the competing sensations eagerly: the warmth of exotically scented air, sensual on her skin; the vibrant jungle greens, threaded through with such an abundance of brilliant, colored flowers that she hardly knew where to look; the startling black of the lava rock in the construction of a low wall, whispering to her of things ancient and mystical.

But it was two in the morning. She was sitting on an uncomfortable wooden bench just outside the main doors of the Lihue Airport. Inside was chaos, as frustrated passengers felt the ripple effect of travel disruptions on the mainland. They were dealing with changing schedules and canceled flights as planes that were supposed to have arrived here were stuck somewhere else in a giant chain reaction.

The driver, Keona, who had been sent for Meg from the Hale Iwa Kai Resort, had taken one look at her face and, despite looking exhausted himself, had gently removed her luggage tags from her hand and shooed her outside.

Any eagerness she had felt about her first ever trip to Hawaii had been tempered two days ago when sudden winter storms in the East had sent North American air travel into a state of absolute meltdown.

Rerouted for the third time, Meg had found herself stranded at a medium-sized Midwestern airport, staring out at where a runway had been totally erased by the blizzard unfolding outside the huge windows.

It had occurred to her, looking out into the impenetrable white of the storm, that she was going to miss the wedding.

And the awful truth of that?

She had been relieved.

The truth was her trepidation had always outweighed her eagerness to see Hawaii.

It wasn't that she didn't want to be with her best friend, Caylee Van Houtte, as she exchanged vows with billionaire Jonathon Winston, at a wedding luau at the exclusive and very private Hale Iwa Kai boutique resort on Kauai.

How could Meg not want that, when she had never seen her best friend so deliriously happy? The wedding had been over eighteen months in the making—even if you had access to unlimited funds, which Jonathon Winston did, you didn't book all the beach cottages at Hale Iwa Kai on a whim.

No, it wasn't that she didn't want to share those moments with Caylee and Jonathon.

It wasn't that at all.

And it wasn't that she had a travel curse—a broken foot in Paris, food poisoning in Thailand, hypothermia in Switzerland—that could raise its ugly head at any time.

It was that Meg didn't want to see her nearly ex-husband, Morgan Hart. They'd been separated eight months now, and every time she contemplated the failure of her marriage it felt as if she was being swallowed by a darkness so suffocating Meg did not know how it was possible to survive.

And, of course, she was going to see Morgan.

For the first time. After the split, she had quietly packed her bags and moved half a country away from him, from the Canadian city of Vancouver, British Columbia, to Ottawa, Ontario.

It had been best. A clean cut. Absolutely no chance of running into him.

But now, he was the best man to Meg's maid

of honor. She thought maybe he was seeing someone. She hadn't been able to bring herself to ask Caylee if he was bringing someone to the wedding with him. But surely Caylee would have mentioned it?

Morgan and Jonathon had been best friends—as had she and Caylee—since they were children.

It was Meg who had introduced Caylee to Jonathon.

But how could she possibly see Morgan again without her heart breaking in two? Without falling at his feet and begging for a different finish? For a happy ending?

Particularly against the backdrop of a wedding? Even though it would be totally different than their own quiet, private nuptials had been, how could the romantically charged event not fill Meg with memories of that moment when she and Morgan had exchanged their own vows?

Believing, naively as it turned out, in forever.

Stop it, Meg ordered herself.

She'd had only a few winks of sleep in the last forty-eight hours. It was just the utter bone-melting exhaustion that was making her feel as if she couldn't do this. Hadn't she been rehearsing for the fact she could not possibly avoid seeing Morgan at the wedding every single day since she had left him?

Meg was positive she had the cool look down pat, the tilt of her chin, the proud set of her shoulders.

He would never, ever know she still loved him, would always love him.

Morgan would never ever know that she still woke in the night reaching for him, that when she realized he was not there she would cry herself back to sleep.

He would never know how, in moments of utter weakness, she would go through her phone, looking at the photos, touching his face, recalling every detail of him, including how his skin felt under her fingertips, or how the memory of his scent haunted her and filled her with a longing, a hunger, that could never be satiated.

And he would never ever know the reason she had left him.

Meg snapped out of her thoughts when Keona, in his bright Hawaiian shirt, came out through the airport doors and gave her a sympathetic look.

For a moment, Meg thought her travel curse might manifest itself as no luggage. How could her bags have possibly followed her through all the changes in flight plans? Added to the travel delays, that should cover her travel curse for Hawaii, shouldn't it? What a relief it would be, if the curse played out early, so as not to disrupt the wedding.

But, no, her luggage was trundling obediently along behind Keona.

The reason for his sympathetic look must be that her tormented thoughts about Morgan were written all over her.

Though even without the thoughts, Meg was pretty sure she cut a pathetic picture, well deserving of pity. She had caught a glimpse of herself in a restroom mirror, and it wasn't good. She was white with exhaustion, her clothes were crumpled, there was a coffee stain on her pale pink shirt, her blond hair had long since escaped any attempts to tame it, what was left of her makeup was worthy of a horror film and she was pretty sure she smelled.

She sighed and followed Keona to the sleek, black limousine that waited. He held open the rear door for her, then stowed her luggage in the trunk. Meg settled into the back seat. It was, of course, pure luxury with deep leather, cool, fragrant air, a sound system, a bar.

It was a reminder of the life she'd had, ever so briefly, then turned her back on.

The car's powerful engine purred as it pulled smoothly away from the curb. Even though it was night, Meg wanted so badly to catch glimpses of this mystical island she found herself on. She peered out the tinted window, but all she could see was a star-studded sky and palm trees swaying gently in silhouette against it.

Soon, lulled by the lack of view, by the night, by the soft, soothing tones of the ukulele music, by the cool embrace from the vehicle's air-conditioning, Meg gave in to her utter and complete weariness. Her eyes fluttered shut.

And did not open again until a soft voice pulled her from the astonishing deepness of her sleep.

"Mrs. Hart."

For a moment, her eyes stayed closed. Maybe it was the most delicious of dreams and she still was Mrs. Hart.

But no, she opened her eyes and Keona was leaning in the back door, regarding her with soft brown eyes. She should really tell him that she wasn't Mrs. Hart anymore.

But technically, she still was. No divorce papers had been signed. In fact, she couldn't even make herself look at the thick separation agreement that had arrived from a well-known Vancouver law firm.

Still, it seemed as if correcting Keona about her marital status presented complexities she didn't really want to get into with strangers, kind as their eyes might be!

"We are very tired," he said, and she realized he was referring not only to her, but also to himself.

Meg did her best to shake herself awake and then scrambled sleepily out of the car. Keona assembled her luggage, carry case expertly fastened to roller suitcase, and it rattled along behind him as he entered a softly lit and completely empty open-air lobby.

Even though she had been Mrs. Hart for two years, Meg had never really become accustomed to the tastefully luxurious spaces of the world that welcomed the very wealthy.

The lobby of Hale Iwa Kai was such a place.

She was too tired to totally appreciate the powerful pillars that supported the soaring architecture of an impossibly high ceiling. The space contained a scattering of deep, inviting couches; oil paintings depicting Hawaiian historic events; huge wooden carved bowls; an entire wooden outrigger canoe.

"It's been a crazy day," Keona told her, quietly, conversationally, as they walked out of the lobby, past a lava-rock wall with water trickling melodically and soothingly down its rough face. "So many flights canceled. We have guests who were supposed to leave today and couldn't. Thankfully, some incoming flights have also been delayed, so we've been able to accommodate everyone. But we are tired."

She followed him through a passageway, over a bridge that spanned a lit pond constructed of the same dark, rich lava rock of the water wall they had gone by. She caught a glimpse of fish darting through turquoise waters.

The passageway opened to a wide path, as black as a lava flow, flanked on both sides by burning tiki torches and hibiscus, the pink blossoms the size of dessert plates. An exotic scent tickled her nose, a combination of the gases being burned by the torches and the perfumes from the flowers.

Curving walkways meandered off the main sidewalk, and at the end of each of those walkways she caught glimpses of nearly hidden cottages.

They weren't, of course, what most people would think of as a cottage, but people like Jonathon Winston and Morgan Hart were not most people. The white stand-alone buildings were spacious and whispered of opulence, with their steep, pitched beam roofs, lush landscaping and oversize stone urn fountains bubbling quiet welcome at each exquisitely carved wooden door.

The resort was slumbering. Except for the insistent call of a night bird, the slap of waves on a yet unseen shoreline, the whisper of Keona's sandals and the sound of her suitcase wheels rumbling along the walkway, it was completely silent.

Finally, Keona chose one of the pathways and followed its winding route through exotic shrubbery to a front door that was as much a work of art as an entryway.

A large stone urn fountain bubbled there. It had a word subtly engraved on it.

Huipu.

"Welcome to Huipu," he said, and quietly opened the door. Meg noticed it was not locked as Keona set her suitcase inside, then bowed slightly to her.

"What does the name mean?" she asked, curious despite how tired she was.

"Unite. Together. We are delighted to host many, many weddings here. We sometimes use this cottage for honeymoons if the main one is already in use."

Meg and Morgan had honeymooned in Paris. After she had broken her foot, on their second day there, he had promised a redo one day. It was possible they could have ended up in a place very like this one.

Keona nodded toward a fierce-looking carved wooden tiki that was nestled in the greenery beside the fountain.

"Lono, ancient god of fertility," he said, and

then added, teasingly, "Don't touch, unless you want a baby."

Her fingers started itching. She had to anchor them on her pocketbook to keep from reaching out.

"May your stay be blessed with much *aloha*," he said.

"Aloha?" she asked, faintly confused. "Isn't that hello?"

"So many things," he said, his tired eyes twinkling. "Hello. Goodbye. And so much more. You'll see." And then he left her.

Alone, Meg hesitated for a moment, and then gave in to the desire to reach out. She rested her hand against Lono's wooden chest. The surface was surprisingly warm, as if it held the heat of the day within it.

"Where were you when I needed you?" she asked, then drew her hand away. It was too late and she could not afford to indulge what-ifs. Not when she would be seeing Morgan tomorrow.

Meg stepped inside the door and felt for a light switch. Instead of an overhead light coming on, two floor lamps blinked to life and bathed the space in a golden glow.

The room was soothing and sumptuous, with dark beams on the high ceiling and wide-plank wooden floors that seemed to glow from within. A huge ceiling fan turned lazily. The furnishings were exquisitely Hawaiian—beautiful wood tables, and rattan couches and chairs, their deep cushions upholstered in subtle tropical prints.

Meg could see a wall-to-wall, floor-to-ceiling bank of windows, opened, at the back of the room. The open windows, like the unlocked door, gave her a sense of being in an utterly safe space. The scent of the sea poured in on the gentle breeze that lifted white gauzy curtains.

Her whole apartment—with its three locks on the door—would have fit into one corner of this "cottage."

While it was unmistakably high-end, Huipu was unlike some of the expensive accommodations she had enjoyed as Mrs. Hart. This space was cozy and comfortable, a place where one could relax with a good book.

While she was trying to hide out from Morgan and recovering from whatever disaster struck this time!

Stop being superstitious, Meg chided herself, the woman who had just longingly touched Lono's chest. She promised herself tomorrow she would give this gracious, inviting space the appreciation it deserved.

Tonight, she wanted only to return to the deep sleep she'd had a tantalizing taste of in the luxurious back seat of the limousine.

CHAPTER TWO

MEG NOTICED THERE was only one door, slightly ajar, off the living room, and she tugged her suitcase along behind her and went through it.

It opened into a spa-like bathroom, and through a door on the other side of it, she caught a glimpse of the foot of a bed.

Tired as she was, she could not resist the shower.

She tore off her rumpled, stained clothing, adjusted the tap, and stepped under it. Water fell on her from the ceiling and sprayed out from the walls. It was like being drenched in a sudden tropical cloudburst. The soap and the shampoo were as wonderfully fragrant and as subtly sensual as the Hawaiian air.

Feeling deliciously clean, she stepped out, regarded her suitcase for a moment and decided she simply did not have the energy to rummage through it in search of pajamas. Tonight, she would live boldly, and sleep naked, the cool, ocean-fresh breeze playing across her clean skin.

Meg wrung the water out of her hair with a thick white towel, and then wrapped another one around herself.

She stepped into the darkness of the bedroom. The bed, ever so faintly illuminated from the large open patio doors beside it, looked to be an antique piece, its pineapple-engraved posters reaching toward the dark beams of a high, open ceiling identical to the one in the living area.

The bed was huge and inviting, and she stepped over to it, dropped the towel and turned back the sheet.

And then froze as her tired mind tried to grapple with the complete shock of her discovery.

Her Hawaii disaster had struck!

There was someone in her bed!

Meg bit back her first inclination, which was to scream. Instead, she swallowed hard and tried to force her tired mind to fit the available information together, like a clumsy child trying to make sense of the scrambled pieces of a jigsaw puzzle.

It was not, she reasoned with herself, placing her hand over the hard beating of her heart, as if she'd encountered a stranger with a knife, intent on evil things, in a back alley in a bad neighborhood.

It's better to be naked in a remote tropical cottage with a stranger? another part of her mind chided.

Meg forced herself to be rational, which was not easy at nearly three in morning, in a place that, for all its enchantment, seemed as foreign to her as the face of the moon.

But, obviously, a mistake had been made. That was all. It wasn't a disaster. It was a human error. So far, no harm done.

Trying to be as quiet as possible, she hooked the dropped towel with her toe, crossed her arms over herself and scuttled a few steps backward toward the bathroom, her suitcase and the exit of Huipu.

But then she froze. A familiar scent tickled at her nose.

Clean.

Delicious.

Sensual.

It was, of course, the scent of the very same shampoo and soap she had just used.

But there were other notes to it. Deeper.

Masculine.

Unmistakable.

Morgan.

And her relief that he was alone in that bed was abject.

Her sleep-deprived mind fumbled to the conclusion that *now* disaster was imminent. Still, it could be averted if Meg backed out of the room as quickly and quietly as possible.

But as her eyes adjusted to the dark and she drank in the familiar lines of him, her husband, Morgan Hart, she was utterly paralyzed with longings as exotic, as mystical, as powerful as the land she found herself in.

Instead of doing the rational thing and making her escape, she drank him in. Her sense of safety, of just a few moments ago, abandoned her. She was aware of danger snapping in the air. And still, she could not make herself back away.

Morgan was sleeping on his belly, his head resting on a crisp, white pillow, his face turned toward her. His elbow was bent, one hand resting up beside his cheek on the linen of the pillowcase. He looked as if he was as naked as she was, though a sheet—that could have been mistaken for a stripe of moonlight—was draped over a narrow band of his hip and bottom.

She felt her mouth go dry as she took in the familiar wideness of his shoulders and the broadness of his back. Her eyes followed the graceful line of his spine, took in the jut of ribs, drifted down the beautiful narrowing of his back to where there were two identical impressions— dimples—just before the sheet-covered curve of his buttocks. His skin was flawless and it glowed like alabaster in the faint light.

The sight of him caused her to remember the

heated silk feel of Morgan's body beneath her fingertips with such raw wanting that it jarred her.

There was a sound. The faintest of sighs, and her eyes flew to his face. It was framed in a tumble of sleep-tousled curls. His hair was the color of the golden sand they had once seen on a beach in New Zealand—where she had been so bitten by sand flies she'd had to see a doctor for prescription antihistamine.

His eyelashes, thick as sooty chimney brushes, swept down over the high cut of perfect cheekbones. His nose was ever so slightly crooked from where it had been broken during a rugby match in his youth.

Meg remembered running her fingertips over that thin white line of a scar the night they had first kissed, fascinated, sensing how the scar told of the warrior in Morgan. And, of course, she found out he was just that, a man who had faced incredible battles in his life with formidable courage.

Don't look at his lips, she ordered herself, but it was too late for orders. Her senses had been in full mutiny since she had realized it was him in that bed.

Now, she surrendered to taking in the line of his lips, full, faintly parted, the bottom one puffy, with that little line down the middle of it…

The taste of his mouth was as sharp in her

memory as if the last time she had kissed him was yesterday, not months ago.

It seemed like a cruel jest of the universe—a terrible twist on her travel curse—that she had arrived in a paradise, at a place called Huipu, to find the man she still loved, naked in bed.

It seemed even more cruel that the cottage was guarded by the god of fertility when she had been unable to make a baby with this man.

Meg stopped herself from going down that road. She needed to solve the problem of the here and now.

It was probably the most natural of mistakes on the part of the resort.

He was Mr. Hart.

The staff, as Keona had told her, thought she was Mrs. Hart, which technically, she still was. They had paired them together, assuming they were husband and wife, and put them in the same cottage. Why wouldn't they?

But Morgan never even had to know about the error.

Meg could still avert disaster if she did the right thing. She took another tiny step backward, practically holding her breath so as not to make a sound and wake him.

Except at that moment, his eyes flicked open. And he looked at her with a look she remembered so well. That she longed for in her dreams.

When Morgan looked at Meg, those brown eyes—the color of exotic coffee, no cream, sprinkled through with gold flecks of stardust—were drowsy with welcome, as if he could not believe his good luck in waking to her.

The look she had seen every single day of their married life.

But then, abruptly, the sleepy welcome left his face, and his brows lowered down over eyes that darkened to a shade beyond black. His eyes suddenly flashed with anything but tenderness. His beautiful mouth turned down in an angry slash.

"What the—" he demanded. He used a word she had only heard him use twice, and one of those times had been when her travel curse had been a purse snatching—her purse that is—in a busy San Francisco coffee shop.

Meg suddenly became aware of the warm air of the tropical night on her body, and realized she was standing before Morgan, dressed in only moonlight!

Now was not the time to remember how comfortable they had once been with these kind of married-couple intimacies.

Meg reached out and yanked the sheet off of him, pulling it to cover herself. Unfortunately, that left Morgan as naked as she had just been. The gorgeous, chiseled lines of his bare buttocks were something artists tried to capture in stone.

And while she was no Michelangelo, she was, after all, an artist.

Morgan didn't know what had awoken him. A scent maybe.

More likely an instinct.

Still, opening his eyes to see Meg standing by the bed, as unclothed as Eve in the garden, her damp hair falling over the swell of her breasts, just like a statue they had seen on their honeymoon in Paris, was one of the shocks of his life.

It felt as if an earthquake—not unheard of here in the Hawaiian Islands—magnitude at least seven point zero, was rocking his world.

Though for one blissful millisecond, he thought he had awoken from the nightmare of the last eight months.

He hoped he had dreamed *them*, those months, and that she'd really been here, all along, looking at him with *that* light softening her eyes.

That light. The one he had waited for his entire life.

The one that said, despite it all, life could be good again.

The one that said, You are loved. You are cherished. I am yours. And you are mine. Forever.

But that feeling lasted only a second, and then

he came fully awake, and fully aware *forever* was the biggest lie of all, a lesson a man should take seriously the first time, after tragedy had stripped everything from him.

He felt a surge of anger that he found himself in a tug-of-war over a sheet with the woman who had never loved him at all, no matter what he thought he saw in her face.

The woman who had destroyed him, already torn asunder by tragedy, all over again, by making him think she was something she wasn't. Meg had had made Morgan believe, however briefly, that in each other, they had found what every single person on the planet searched for.

The sanctuary of love.

A sanctuary he had once had, and longed for so completely, that it had made him vulnerable to what he thought Meg had offered.

Well, he would be vulnerable no more.

Morgan conceded the sheet to her and leaped out of the bed from the other side. With his back to her, he found a damp towel he had left on the floor the night before. He wrapped it around his waist and then spun around and glared at his soon-to-be ex-wife across the width of the bed.

Because it was over, even if the separation agreement remained unsigned by both of them.

"What the hell are you doing in here?" he snapped.

Meg flinched from his tone, but he steeled himself to her wounded look. She had done this, not him.

"I… I… I think the resort made a mistake," she stammered. "Because of the last names…"

Her voice drifted away.

Hotel errors seemed ridiculously small in the face of the larger question, which had haunted him for months.

Why?

Morgan wanted to demand to know *why* and not just about the lack of final signatures on divorce documents either.

Why, when they had experienced what he would have called two blissful years of marriage had Meg suddenly pulled the plug? She hadn't even had the courtesy to tell him in person.

An apartment that he had felt the emptiness of even before he found her note.

Couldn't adjust to the lifestyle.

It was useless to wonder what it was beyond her ridiculously short explanation. Hadn't he gone over it a million times in the past eight months? No answers from his silent, absent wife.

Maybe it was just that simple. She couldn't handle the lifestyle.

How lucky did a man have to be to find the one woman on the earth who could not adjust to being wealthy beyond her wildest dreams?

CHAPTER THREE

H<small>OW LUCKY DID</small> a man have to be, Morgan asked himself, to find the one woman who couldn't adjust to a honeymoon in Paris, a week in Thailand on business, a spontaneous trip to New Zealand, a weekend shopping trip to San Francisco?

How lucky did a man have to be to find the one woman who couldn't adjust to a penthouse in Vancouver's tony English Bay? Couldn't adjust to exquisite meals, fine jewelry, great cars, use of a private jet, backstage passes to some of the most coveted events in the world?

Fresh anger was clawing at his throat as he regarded Meg, tucking that sheet around her as if she was a model waiting to be painted.

She looked like a goddess, standing there in the faint light, draped in swaths of the sheet and moonlight. She was so beautiful. Her eyes were her most arresting feature, even now, when she was freshly scrubbed of makeup.

Maybe especially now, her beauty so natural. Her eyes were wide, fringed in a natural abundance of thick lashes, the color a deep, mossy green that was ever changing, one minute dark, the next sparking with light. Intelligence. Inquisitiveness. Mischief.

Desire.

Morgan could not think of that right now, with only a towel and a sheet between their total nakedness. Instead, he completed his inventory of her, trying to be dispassionate. But it was hard to be that when he had tasted every inch of her from her high cheekbones, to the sweet little lobes of her ears, to the button of her nose and to the full sensual swell of her lips, the hollows of her collarbone.

Her breasts, her belly button, her toes...

The weakness—and heat—of those memories crumpled his defenses as much as being woken in the middle of the night by his unclothed ex had.

The slight lowering of his barriers allowed Morgan to see how tired Meg was, swaying with exhaustion, her skin frighteningly pale.

She was thinner, he noted, her cheeks more hollow and her collarbones sticking out, her shoulders fragile. Her eyes—those glorious eyes—looked bigger in her thinner face, and had dark circles under them.

They were a green that had always felt to him

as if they held the calm of a deep pool on a summer day, but tonight they were shadowed.

With some secret sorrow.

He shook off his intense *need* to know what that was, and what part it had played in the demise of their marriage. She'd had eight months to confide in him, but no, not a word from her. Just packed her bag and disappeared from his life as if what they had shared had meant nothing and been nothing.

"Where's your girlfriend?" she asked stiffly, as if a man abandoned by his wife had somehow betrayed *her* by seeking comfort elsewhere.

And while there had not been a word from Meg about anything, she knew about that? Of course she would know. She and his best friend's fiancée, Caylee, were also best friends.

And yet Caylee had not shed any light on Megan's sudden abandonment of the marriage. If anything, she seemed as distressed and shocked by it as he himself was.

"None of your business," he snapped at Meg, but felt no satisfaction at all when his arrow landed and she flinched from it.

Why not protect himself by letting Meg believe he had moved on?

The truth was the relationship with Marjorie had been as brief and disastrous as might be expected of a rebound. It had never progressed beyond a few casual dates, though he might have led Caylee to believe otherwise.

There had never been anything approaching intimacy, and not because Marjorie had been unwilling.

The truth was, he couldn't be intimate with someone else when he still felt intensely connected to the woman who had left him.

He had probably only accepted Marjorie's invitation to go out because Morgan had known word would get back to Meg that he had moved on, and swiftly, too.

It had been childish. It had reminded him of a group of boys in middle school, the tough kids who had played a game where one held a match and the other held his palm above it.

Unflinching, looking directly in the other person's eyes.

Giving a message. *No matter what you do, you can't hurt me.*

"She's not coming to the wedding?" Meg asked, even though he couldn't have been any clearer than *none of your business.*

"No," he snapped.

"Does she like children?" Meg asked.

"What?" He was not sure this middle-of-the-night conversation could get any crazier.

"Marjorie. Does she like children?"

"For God's sake, Meg, how do I know? Why would I care?"

She got a pinched look about her, apparently unwilling to accept that this also fell solidly into the none-of-her-business category.

"Our immediate problem is accommodation. I'll go sort it out at the front desk," he told Meg coolly, moving toward the door.

"No, no. I can go. You were here first. I mean, there is no one at the desk. I just came by there, but I'll figure out something."

He turned and looked back at her.

"It's my curse," she said, "not yours."

She was trying, even above her weariness, to insert a bit of levity. Instead, it reminded him of her propensity for calamity, which he had to admit he had found mostly adorable.

It had always made him feel protective of her. And it did that now, too.

His wife. His forever.

He was not sure he could trust himself with the sudden surge of anger he felt, but still, just like those boys in the schoolyard, he wasn't going to flinch from holding his hand over the flame.

Morgan wasn't giving Meg the satisfaction of knowing how destroyed he was. He'd hold his hand above her flame until it blistered before he would let her know how badly she was hurting him.

"I'll take care of it," he said firmly, and when she went to protest, he held up his hand with all the authority of someone who ran a billion-dollar company. "We'll sort it out in the morning. You take the bed. I'll take the couch."

Not once, in their entire marriage, had they gone to bed so angry with each other that one of them slept on the couch.

"I can take the couch," she said, chewing her lip, apparently not getting it that he was the boss—of course, when had she ever?

Hadn't that been one of the things that delighted him? How she didn't seem impressed by what he was? How, instead, she had seen *who* he was.

But in the end, *what* he was was apparently more than she could handle.

Besides which, he did not want to be thinking of one single thing about his wife that had delighted him.

"I can sleep in a lounge chair by the pool," she suggested, always creative. "Or go find Caylee."

He shot her a look. "Whatever our differences are, we are not going to let them ruin this for Cay and Jon."

Her mouth fell open and her eyes darkened. "As if I would!"

"Once," he said, and heard the weariness in his own voice, "I would have believed that. Back when I thought I knew who you were."

He saw the arrow had landed, again, and again Morgan took no satisfaction from the wounded look it provoked.

"This is their time," he said sternly.

"You don't have to tell me that!"

"Then let's not begin with an argument," Morgan said smoothly.

"It's not an argument. It's a discussion."

"Whatever it is, it's the middle of the night and I don't want to have it. You take the bed."

Before she could press further, he went out the door that led to the bathroom and shut it behind him. He walked past her unopened suitcase. He went through the door that adjoined the living room and closed it with a little more snap than was strictly necessary.

He might have thought he got in the last word.

However, a moment later that adjoining door whispered open. Meg had divvied up the bedding and she dumped a pile outside the door. She did it so quickly that he hardly caught a glimpse of her, except to see she was still swaddled in the sheet.

Then he heard her, on the other side of that door, deciding—too late, really—to dig through her luggage and presumably come up with some pajamas.

He gathered up the bedding she had tossed him—a thin blanket and a pillow. He folded the blanket in half lengthwise and put it on the couch. He let the damp towel drop and climbed between the rough fold of his makeshift bed.

He was still naked and didn't have a single piece of clothing out here with him. It was all in the bedroom, which he heard Meg make her way back into.

But he'd be damned if he was begging her for a pair of undershorts to wear to protect his modesty in the morning. Because once you started begging a woman like her, there was really no telling where it was going, or where it would end.

Morgan set the alarm on his watch, since his phone was still on the bedside table beside Meg.

He would not think of her lying in that bed. He just wouldn't. He had practical matters to turn his mind to.

For instance, what time would the lobby open? Six? It looked as if Meg needed to sleep for a week—Caylee had been reporting on her travel adventures—so he could sneak in the bedroom in the morning, get some clothes and get the accommodation kerfuffle sorted out before she was even awake.

He needn't have worried about setting his alarm though, because an entire army of Kauai's roosters began to raucously welcome the day before first light had even stained the sky.

Not that it mattered.

Morgan had not slept a wink since he had laid eyes on his beautiful wife and recognized from the ache in his heart that, despite it all, he loved her still.

A secret he was never, ever sharing with her. He would not be foolish enough, weak enough to hand Megan Hart, his wife, the weapons to wound him again.

Not even if, in that first unguarded moment, when they had looked at each other for the first time in eight months, he felt as if he had seen some truth in her eyes, too.

The kind of truth that could make a man beg.

If he let himself be weak. Which Morgan Hart had absolutely no intention of being. Ever. Again.

CHAPTER FOUR

MEG OPENED HER EYES.

It sounded as if a thousand roosters were crowing right outside her window with joyous enthusiasm. Other birds joined in—*ooh-hoo, ooh-hoo*—a contest for superiority in the decibel department.

Though Meg had never actually been to a jungle, the exotic cacophony of sound seemed identical to movies she had seen with that setting.

As she woke up more, she became aware of the sensation of the sheets against her skin, a luxurious feel that only fabrics with impossibly high thread counts had. Sunlight, filtered through swaying pond fronds, poured through the windows and dappled the bed. A warm, scented breeze caressed her skin. She felt something she had not felt for a very long time.

Sensuous.

As if she'd been sleeping and something about this enchanted place was coaxing her back to life.

Beneath *that* feeling was one equally as astonishing. Could it really be?

Happiness.

Meg had not woken up feeling happy for eight full months. In fact, she had woken each and every morning since she had left Morgan with the same sense of crushing despondency.

Morgan.

Was her close encounter of the unexpected kind with her nearly ex-husband the reason for the happiness that was unfurling in her like a sail catching the wind?

The fact that he'd been alone in the bed?

Of course it wasn't!

Their encounter had been tense. Awkward. He had been angry.

No, who wouldn't be happy to wake up in paradise?

The sensuality was not so easily attributed to the enchantment of Hawaii. She stretched, aware of her body, breath and muscle, strength and grace.

Sensual. And maybe not happiness, precisely. Contentment. Which had a steadiness to it that made it seem even better than happiness, that elusive force that came and went with every shift in the wind.

But, no, it wasn't anything quite as staid as contentment. It was happiness, and there was no lying to herself. It was sharing a world with

Morgan—even if he was angry—that caused it. His scent still lingered on the sheets, for heaven's sake. It would be pathetic to draw the bedding in close to her nose and inhale as if it was a drug, but she did that anyway.

She closed her eyes. Breathed deeply. Then frowned. Of course, there was the problem of him not knowing if his new lady friend liked children. Acting as if it didn't matter.

What was all this for, if he got involved with a woman who wasn't going to give him a family?

She had tried to ask Caylee, subtly, if Morgan seemed serious about Marjorie. How dysfunctional was this? Being worried about the quality of your ex's new relationship?

Caylee didn't know. She and Jonathon had only met Marjorie once, by chance. There had been no couples activities.

Was that good or bad? What right did she have to feel relieved that Morgan was not sharing *their* friends with his new woman?

She breathed in the scent on the sheet again. *Morgan.*

"What are you doing?"

Meg's eyes snapped open. And there he was, in the flesh, her husband. Not that she wanted to be thinking about his flesh. And the way it had looked last night, turned to silvered, sensual marble by moonlight.

There was that word again. *Sensual*. There could not be a doubt left where *that* association was coming from. Meg felt heat rise in her cheeks.

She dropped the sheet from her nose, but only to her chin. Even though she was in perfectly decent pajamas.

Too decent. Unsuited for the tropics. It occurred to her she didn't want Morgan to see her rather frumpy choice of nightwear: light blue trousers, a button-up shirt top.

Meg didn't want him to know how far she had fallen from the woman who had, as his wife, explored an exquisitely feminine side of herself that had been hidden until he had drawn it out. She had given herself over to the delights of her husband finding her sexy. Her nightwear had been as bold and as beautiful as he had made her believe she was.

He moved on, thank goodness, from her sniffing the sheets.

"I have some bad news."

Of course he did! When didn't she have bad news when she traveled?

And yet it felt to Meg as if it didn't matter what he said.

Her husband was in the same room with her. He looked tired after spending the night on the couch and she could see every loss he had ever experienced in the dark shadows of his eyes.

Losses he had trusted her with.

Losses she had thought her love could heal him from.

Until she had discovered that she would be adding another loss to the layers that already existed in those eyes.

Mrs. Hart, the doctor had said, *I'm so sorry to tell you this.*

The secret she had never shared with him, the reason she had made herself say goodbye and put a world between them.

That world between them painfully evident now in the set of his broad shoulders under the bright, tropically patterned shirt he had on, in the way his hands were shoved deep into the pockets of his crisp khaki shorts. Had he come in here while she was sleeping and gathered some clothes? He must have. Had he paused and looked at her, the way she had looked at him last night?

The sun was dancing in the sun-on-sand gold of his curls, and she noticed faint stubble on his chin and cheeks that made her want to run her hand across them, to feel that sensuous roughness under her fingertips.

That scent—that was so purely him, that she

had recognized last night and that he had left on the sheets—tickled her nose.

She closed her eyes for a moment. She could tear down his barriers with a single confession about why she had moved away. The temptation to tell him, to feel his arms fold around her and his tears touch her hair, had to be fought.

"There are no other rooms," Morgan told her, grimly.

"Wh-what?" she stammered.

"From the sound of it, not on the entire island. Air travel is in chaos all over the country. People who were scheduled to leave Kauai haven't been able to get out. I'm shocked that your plane arrived."

Keona had told her this last night, but even when Meg had found Morgan already occupying their cottage, she hadn't linked what he had told her to the consequences.

"We're just going to have to suck it up and figure it out," he told her.

"Figure it out how?" Meg squeaked.

"Look—" Morgan gestured expansively "—it's a suite. It's not like it's a studio. I can take the couch."

There it was again. The most inappropriate reaction to Morgan's bad news.

Happiness.

Of course, it was going to be absolute torment

to share a space with him, to be in such close quarters, to not tell him the truth.

Torment, like someone who had developed a deathly allergy to chocolate finding themselves at an exquisite buffet with one of those chocolate fountains.

You could still enjoy the sight of it.

You could still enjoy the fragrance of it.

Couldn't you?

You just couldn't taste it.

"You're right," she told him, trying to strip every trace of happiness from her voice, trying to sound stoic and resigned, "we'll have to suck it up."

"I don't even know if we should tell Caylee," Morgan said, raking a hand through those tousled curls. "You've arrived now, but her parents aren't here yet. The wedding party clothes were shipped separately and haven't turned up either."

"Her gown?" Meg whispered. Caylee's wedding gown was like something out of a fairy tale. It had been custom made specifically for her by up-and-coming designer Dianne Lawrence. Dianne had taken her inspiration from the dress then–Princess Elizabeth had worn for her wedding to Lieutenant Philip Mountbatten. Each of the thousands of tiny seed pearls had been painstakingly hand stitched.

"That dress cost more than most people's cars," she said, stricken for her friend.

"Oh, yeah," he said, bitterly, "the world you don't want."

That was the lie she had told him. Though not quite a lie. This was what people from humble backgrounds like hers did not know about marrying into extreme wealth: you never quite felt like you belonged. You always felt like the outsider looking in. Meg had felt like a child who had accidentally been seated at the adult table, an imposter waiting to be found out.

Though, not everyone felt that way. Caylee, from the very same wrong-side-of-the-tracks Vancouver neighborhood as Meg, had taken to Jonathon's lifestyle and wealth like the proverbial duck to water, delighting in every moment of it.

Still, practical Meg wondered if the dress was insured. Good grief, could you insure wedding dresses?

"What about everything else?" she whispered. "All of it."

"The whole wedding party's clothes?" She thought of how she and Caylee had chosen the colors for the bridesmaid dresses, a green so dark it was almost black, so that it wouldn't compete in photos with the amazing colors and beauty of the location.

She thought of the painstaking custom tailoring that had gone into each of the men's lightweight summer suits. You did not just replace that!

"But the wedding is in three days!" she exclaimed.

Morgan lifted a shoulder, reminding her he was a man who had been battered relentlessly by life. On the scale of catastrophe, missing clothing, even for the wedding of the century, would barely register with him.

But the distress her best friend must be feeling pushed Meg's own chaotic emotions—thankfully—into the background.

"I'll go see her right away." Of course, she didn't move, still unwilling to let Morgan see her in the I've-given-up-on-life pajamas.

"Good idea. There is a breakfast buffet set up by the main pool for the wedding party."

"The main pool? How many pools are there?"

"That creek that meanders through the property joins half a dozen or so pools together. It's quite amazing. They're all so unique." For a moment, he looked wistful, and Meg wondered if Morgan was thinking of the days when they would have delighted in exploring such a space as Hale Iwa Kai Resort together.

But then the handsome features of his face hardened.

"Go left out the front door to the main pool. There's one you probably don't want to end up at. It's—"

He hesitated.

"It's what?"

He looked pained. "Not where breakfast is," he said gruffly. And then he was gone.

And even though everything was the same, including the sunbeam that danced across her bed, it felt as if he had taken the light from the room with him.

Meg was aware, as she chose an outfit and dressed, that she had prepared her tropical wardrobe with Morgan in mind. The choices had seemed unbelievably difficult. She was the one who had walked out on the marriage, so it would have seemed like the worst kind of mixed message to wear things that made it seem as if she was trying to attract him.

Or compete with his new friend.

So she had selected fade-into-the-background knee-length shorts and practical cotton blouses. Looking at herself in the mirror, she swept her hair back, clipped it into a messy bun and then sighed heavily.

In her beige shorts and paisley-patterned shirt, she looked as if she'd been inspired by the fashion sense of women who showed dogs and had only one desire—and that was for the dog to be the star of the show! Just like the pajamas, she suddenly didn't want Morgan to see her in an unflattering light. Particularly since his new friend wasn't here.

She reminded herself, firmly, this wasn't about her. Or Morgan.

It was about Caylee and Jonathon, and building toward a perfect wedding day for them. That focus was even more necessary now that there were some obstacles to overcome.

Meg noticed the blouse, which she had never worn because it had been purchased for this occasion, still had the price tag on it. She went into the kitchen area, marveling at the beauty and finishes of Huipu. The stocked wine cooler and the coffee bar with its barista-worthy machine she understood, but who on earth used a stand mixer whilst on vacation? In Hawaii?

A quick perusal of the drawers, and she found scissors and dispensed with the tag. And then, unable to stop herself, she took the scissors into the bathroom, took off the shorts and cut three inches off of the legs on both sides. She unraveled the fabric to give the hem a frayed look.

When she put the shorts back on, she was pleased. Her impromptu alteration had resulted in a bohemian look. Meg accentuated that look by undoing the bottom buttons of the shirt and tying it in a knot, exposing her midriff.

She eyed herself critically.

Too much?

Oh, no. So much better! As she walked out of the cottage, she was aware of the feeling of the warm air on her bare midriff, and also of a lightness in her step that she had not had in it for eight months.

She was not at all sure how wise it was, but she was definitely stepping away from the dowdy, heartbroken, nearly divorced image she had been wallowing in!

It felt as if Meg took in the resort, in daylight, with that same lightness of spirit her change of outfit had given her. Her senses felt wide open as she breathed in the utter enchantment of a resort where every single detail had been designed to showcase Hawaii's incredible beauty.

CHAPTER FIVE

"MEG!"

As her best friend folded her arms around her, Meg felt a deep sense of homecoming. Caylee stepped back, her hands still resting on Meg's shoulders.

They took each other in with deep appreciation, sisters of the heart, reunited. Though almost identical in height and stature, in every other way their appearances were opposite. Caylee was as dark as Meg was blonde; she kept her hair short, in a pixie style that few could pull off but that she did.

Meg was so pleased to see how relaxed Caylee looked, radiating the well-being of a woman loved.

For a moment, Meg thought her friend was going to comment on her weight loss, the shadows under her eyes, but she didn't. Cay sighed happily.

"I am so glad you made it. I was so worried about you getting here. I couldn't do this without you."

"I think you should be more worried about your parents not being here. And the lost wedding clothes. Especially your dress!"

"How do you know about that?"

"Oh." Meg hoped her voice didn't sound strangled. "I, um, ran into Morgan."

"You did?" Caylee breathed hopefully. "How did that go?"

Cay's wish—that they had thrown themselves into each other's arms, and that they were magically and completely reconciled—was naked in her voice.

Her wedding was in three days! She had other things to worry about.

"It was okay," Meg said.

"Oh."

"You must be sick about the entire wedding party wardrobe being missing," Meg said to change the subject.

"Oh." Caylee waved her hand as if at a bothersome fly. "It'll turn up."

"Caylee! A little panic might be in order." She held out a finger. "You have today. You have tomorrow. Then, the following day, you have *I do*. Not to mention your missing dress is worth enough to buy a small country."

"It's just a dress."

Just a dress?

"Tell that to someone who didn't get sent twelve

hundred and sixty-two photos of wedding dresses. Who didn't meet you in Montreal—twice—to meet the designer. Who didn't field midnight calls—"

"I forgot the time difference," Caylee wailed.

"Six times!"

"Yes, well," Caylee said, not very apologetically, "the most important thing is that everyone gets here."

"Forty-two virtual meetings with Becky, Allie and Samantha," Meg reminded her. "One trip to Bridesmaid in Manhattan to choose four different styles of dresses that went together, and to finalize the color—"

"The love is the most important part," Caylee said, firmly.

"Who are you and what have you done with Caylee?" Meg asked dryly.

"I know! I was turning into an absolute bridezilla over everything. Why didn't you tell me?" This was said accusingly, and she didn't wait for Meg to answer. "Because you were three thousand miles away, that's why."

Caylee had not approved of Meg's move— or of her leaving Morgan. She had acted as if the move—and the end of her best friend's marriage—was a personal assault on her own hopes and dreams, never mind the wedding plans.

And yet, underneath that, always, the love was there.

The concern.

Meg had not confided the real reason, even to Caylee. It made the burden she carried feel really lonely. For the second time since she'd been here—less than twenty-four hours—she felt an urge to confess all!

"Let's forget about problems for now," Caylee said. She came and stood beside Meg and put her head on her shoulder.

"Can you believe it?" she whispered. "Look at us, two girls from East Vancouver, here."

She made a sweeping gesture with her arm, and Meg took it in. There was a huge turquoise pool with a bridge across it, and a waterfall cascading down at the far end of it, the lush tropical plants around it, the deck loungers under their white canopies.

Leading away from the pool was a wide path that opened onto a crescent of golden sand dotted with palm trees and outrigger canoes. The beach looked out onto a protected bay, the natural ombre effect, light blue deepening to navy by the time it reached the mouth, making Meg's artist's heart sigh.

As did all of it. The nearby mountains held the whole resort in a dramatic cup. Their sheer slopes were covered with lush rainforests and bisected by deep fissures and dramatic cliffs. From where the two friends stood, they could see a waterfall spilling down the side of the mountain, with rainbows dancing around it. The waterfall at the resort pool was obviously designed to look like a continuation of that spectacular natural feature.

"You see why I'm not worried about the dress?" Caylee said. "This. It makes me feel small in the best possible way. Like no matter how I try to create beauty, this will be the star of the show. It's a relief to just let go."

Meg could understand that. It had been months of organizing, worrying, ordering, perfecting details, ferreting out what could go wrong.

Everything Caylee could do had been done. It was good that she could let go.

"You're letting type A's everywhere down with this laid-back attitude," Meg teased her.

"You know, Jonathon and I got here three days ago, and I thought I'd get more and more wound up as the wedding approached. That hasn't happened at all. I mean, of course I'm worried about the plane delays, and missing parents and clothing, but in the end? There's absolutely nothing I can do about it."

"That's true," Meg conceded.

"I feel more and more relaxed, like the spirit of *aloha* is contagious."

"Keona mentioned the multiple meanings of *aloha* to me last night."

"It's not really a word," Caylee said, almost dreamily. "It's a feeling. A spirit of love and acceptance, compassion and forgiveness. It's kind of this lovely attitude that permeates *everything*. Like it's the life force and you feel it in every single thing here."

Meg knew artists, and plenty of them. She was used to this kind of talk. But from Caylee, her super-driven friend? It was ever so slightly distressing!

"Do you know what a *shaka* is?" Cay asked.

"A chakra?" Meg asked. Again, it was definitely artist talk. "You're making me nervous, Caylee. Very nervous."

"Not a chakra. A *shaka*. It's used here, almost in place of a wave."

Caylee demonstrated, thumb and pinky extended, remaining three fingers folded into the palm. "It means hang loose, take it easy, everything's fine."

While Caylee's new attitude was all well and good, Meg thought in her position, as maid of honor, she had to step up to the plate, and make some things happen! Somebody had to worry!

"Despite everything being goodness and light," she said carefully, "we still need a backup plan. In case the wedding wardrobe doesn't arrive."

"Of course! I've got it covered. I'm going to send you on a rescue mission today."

Meg pictured herself spending her first day in paradise making endless phone calls trying to track down the shipment of clothing and the missing parents. She actually liked the idea of having a job to do. It would keep her mind off Morgan. And besides, what was to say she couldn't do it from right here, beside the pool?

"Oh, look who's here," Caylee said in a conspiratorial whisper, as if they were still in high school and Bill Fletcher, captain of the football team, whom Meg had harbored a secret crush on, had just entered the room.

So, she knew before turning to see him, who it was. She was aware that Caylee was watching her face, and that she was smiling with satisfaction at whatever she saw there.

"I have to meet with the chef today," Caylee said. "We might have to do a menu change. Ingredients are not showing up."

This was said casually, as if a menu change for dozens and dozens of people was nothing.

"Can you go into town and find some dresses? Just in case?" Caylee said.

"What?"

"A backup plan, just like you said."

"I think a more sensible backup plan would be tracking down the shipment."

"Keona is working on that. Meanwhile, you know all our sizes."

"You want me to pick out a backup wedding gown for you?" Meg asked, horrified. "And bridesmaid dresses?"

"I'm sure we won't need them. Keona seems to be a bit of a miracle worker. But as you say, just in case. Something white for me. Flirty. Fun. Same for the bridesmaids. Not white, of course, but fun. I need your eye for color. Something that will look great in the photos. There're all kinds of cute shops in a little village not far from here. They'll have sundresses galore."

"Sundresses," Meg repeated sadly.

"Well, we'll have to wear something, and there's no way to replace a thirty-thousand-dollar Dianne Lawrence in three days."

"I can check if there's a bridal boutique," Meg said.

"I'll leave it in your capable hands," Caylee decided, way too lightly. "Take him with you. He can be in charge of the backup plan for the groomsmen."

Meg followed Caylee's gaze to where Morgan was helping himself at the buffet. How could guys do that? Load up on the waffles and smother them in syrup and whipped cream and never gain an ounce?

She looked back at her friend and narrowed

her gaze. She actually wondered if the wedding wardrobe was really lost, or this was all an elaborate scheme by Caylee to throw her and Morgan together.

Meg had to nip such reconciliation efforts in the bud.

But suddenly she remembered Morgan warning her not to ruin this for Caylee and Jonathon. Caylee was obviously in the thrall of island enchantment at the moment, but that could change if things went sideways.

It was their wedding and if a backup plan— even a silly one—made the bride-to-be feel better, Meg was just going to have to suck it up.

Besides, maybe it could be an opportunity. To probe, just a little bit about the girlfriend, and find out if she was a suitable replacement.

"Morgan," Caylee called. "I have a job for you."

He ambled over with his carb-laden plate. "Yes?" He was scrupulously ignoring Meg.

"You know how the wedding clothes are lost? Meg had this excellent idea."

This was getting twisted somehow.

"You know how she always has such fun ideas?"

Morgan nodded reluctantly, his eyes on Caylee, sensing the trap.

"She thought she and you should go into town together and get some just-in-case backup clothes."

"Oh," he said. He shot Meg a dark look. He looked as if he was going to protest, and then he swallowed it.

She shook her head, letting him know it wasn't her idea. At all.

"Like what do you mean, backups?" he said.

"Probably something simple for the guys. White shirts? Black trousers? Well, maybe not black. We had gone with white for the custom suits and I don't want you to cook out there on the beach during the ceremony. Maybe shorts? Let Meg decide. She has an eye for these kinds of things."

"Meg has an eye for men in shorts?" he said, and lifted a dark slash of his brow. "Oh, all the things I didn't know."

Caylee laughed way too hard, evidently ignoring the faint bitterness of the final part of his sentence.

"Of course, we need the replacement items today. Because you told us to set aside all day tomorrow for your surprise for the wedding party."

This was the first Meg had heard of Morgan planning a surprise. But then she was hardly in his inner circle anymore.

"Whatever you need, Caylee," he said smoothly.

Caylee beamed at him. It was a statement Meg was pretty sure Morgan was going to regret making, if he didn't already!

CHAPTER SIX

"Do you want to drive, or should I?" Morgan asked Meg. He was sorry they were being sent on this errand together, but he was determined to be civil.

They were standing at a selection of golf carts parked in the shade of a palm tree grove that was tucked away beside the front entrance of the resort. The golf carts were at the beginning of a paved path that would take them to an old sugar mill and plantation village. The buildings now housed boutiques and restaurants.

"I like it that you never assume you're going to drive, just because you're the guy," Meg told him.

The truth was, at this exact point in time, he didn't want Meg to like one single thing about him. It felt as if it wouldn't take much of a push to collapse his defenses completely.

He slid her a look. She was wearing cut-off shorts and a tied-up shirt that showed off the slender lines of both her long legs and flat tummy. She had her hair—each strand a different variation on blonde, from white to gold—scooped up in a clip. He'd always loved her hair, and he had particularly liked it when she wore it like that.

Had he ever told her that?

Would it have made a difference if he had?

Those were the kind of thoughts, Morgan knew, that could torment, if you allowed them to gain traction.

What had he done wrong? How could he have let Meg know, any more than he had, that she was his world, that it felt as if he had needed her as much as air?

And yet, that was untrue, because without air you died, and without Meg? Here he was, surviving. A lesson life had already taught him.

You survived.

He reminded himself to replace all his *what-ifs* with *even-ifs*, a poignant lesson from a long-ago grief counsellor.

What if gave the illusion of control.

Even if acknowledged a kind of powerlessness, a lesson Morgan raged against, even as life showed him over and over—

"Would you drive?" Meg asked. "I just want to soak it all in. You've probably been here before? To Hawaii?"

"No," he said. "Never. Despite what you might

think, rich people don't necessarily jet off to the tropics at every opportunity."

He saw she got his reference immediately. The center of his family for multiple generations had been a cottage on the shores of Okanagan Lake, outside of Kelowna, British Columbia. His great-grandfather had started a lumber company that, in the hands of his grandfather, father, and then him and his brother, had taken the Hart family into the ranks of the world's richest people.

It would have been easy for the Harts to become comfortable with elitist lifestyles: private jets, box seats, the best hotels and vacation spots in the world. It would have been easy to indulge in excess.

But the plain values of his hardworking great-grandfather and great-grandmother had stayed with the family, and grounded them.

And one place, more than any other, was responsible for that.

Named after his great-grandmother, the cottage—Sarah's Reach—was a rambling log structure in British Columbia's interior, sitting on the edge of pristine forest and the immense shore of a deep, mystical lake.

The cottage had been a jumble of styles, a structure that had been added onto a million times, without once having had the benefit of an architectural design, so that it could accommodate an ever-growing family.

In complicated, busy-lives life, it had represented simplicity. It was icy water on summer afternoons, rickety boats with fishing lines dangling from them, the crisp smell of woodsmoke and toasted marshmallows hanging in the air.

Morgan could almost hear his brother laughing, the shrieks of his niece and nephew getting into the water of that lake for the first time in the season...

He realized Meg's hand was resting on his arm, drawing him back from the pain that crept up on him like this sometimes, when he had let his guard down, when he least expected it.

He looked deep into the unbelievable mossy green of those eyes and wanted to fall toward the understanding he saw there.

Instead, he shook off her touch, and swung away from her to the golf cart.

She slid into the seat beside him, and he embarrassed himself by jerking the golf cart violently as he reversed. He was unaccustomed to the pedals, which were touchy.

"It's not your sports car," she said, laughing.

Was that another dig about the lifestyle she had been unable to adjust to? Maybe it would be better not to run every single thing she said through that filter.

On the other hand, maybe that was exactly what he needed to do, because her laughter was like a drug to him, seeping past his defenses, erasing their painful history.

Thankfully, the golf cart required his full focus. With Meg's propensity for disaster, he was glad she had not chosen to drive. The vehicle either responded too much to his foot on the pedal or not at all. The stop-and-go motion left Meg clinging to the support post beside her with both hands, as if her life depended on it, which maybe it did.

A few minutes in, Morgan felt like he might be getting the hang of it, but just when it looked as if maybe they could both relax, a chicken marched out on the path in front of them, forcing him to brake so heavily they both nearly hit their heads on the dashboard.

The chicken paused, did an annoyed tilt of its head and then strutted to the other side of the road.

"Why did the chicken cross the road?" she asked, deadpan.

Only the chicken was not crossing the road. Just as Morgan tried to slide by, it abruptly changed course and came back in front of them, causing him to slam on the brakes again.

"It's a good thing we don't have a windshield,"

he commented, "because I think both our heads would be through it."

"Surprising it didn't happen, given my curse," she said.

He couldn't argue with that! "The day is young," he said.

The chicken squawked its admonishment at him, fanned its wings, cocked its black silky head this way and that, and then tucked its wrinkled stick legs under and plunked itself down right in the center of the path, leaving no way to get around it.

"Is it laying an egg?" Meg asked, after a moment.

"How would I know what it's doing?"

"It's quite pretty, isn't it? Look at how the sun is bringing out a blue hue in the black of his feathers."

"I don't think boys lay eggs," he told her.

She ignored the lesson on the sexing of chickens. "I even see purple."

He remembered this so clearly: how Meg saw the world so differently than anyone he had ever met before. For her, an annoyance on the road became a moment to pause, to look at things more deeply, to notice something she had never noticed before.

"Do I see a chicken in a future art piece?" he asked.

"Possibly," Meg said agreeably.

Morgan found the horn on the cart and tapped it. It made a tiny beep-beep sound. He was not sure if chickens could yawn, but if they could, that one did. Annoyed, Morgan edged up on it.

"Don't run it over!" Meg cried.

"Actually, roast chicken for supper is sounding more appealing by the second."

"I don't think I could eat it now that I've met it."

"*Met* is a bit of a stretch," he noted, even though he was not sure he could eat it now either, having seen the colors of blue and purple sewn amongst its feathers.

"I'm not going to run it over. I'm just showing it it doesn't own the road."

"Showing it who's the boss," she agreed solemnly and then she giggled.

Morgan shot her a warning look.

The chicken apparently disagreed with his assessment of who owned the road, and hers of who the boss was. It tilted its head defiantly, decided he was not threatening and found something interesting to pluck at under its wing.

Morgan wondered if you could come up with an experience more humiliating than being bested by a chicken.

Meg snorted beside him.

He knew that sound well. It was her trying to

hold back laughter. Once, they had attended the art show of an extremely well-known Canadian artist. It had been a mark of how well she was doing in the art world that she had been invited.

They had stood in front of the artist's newest painting, she doing her best to look reverent. She had not been succeeding very well.

Morgan had whispered in her ear, *It looks like a bag of trash a cat got into.*

She had made that exact snorting sound, and then, he'd had to take her out the side exit, and they had stood in the alley beside a bag of trash a cat had gotten into, howling with totally inappropriate laughter.

Small moments. Why were they always the best?

Morgan got out of the golf cart, partly to deal with the chicken, mostly because he did not want to share laughter with her.

He went around the front of the golf cart. He waved his hands at the chicken.

"Shoo," he said.

Nothing.

"Get lost," he said, a little more aggressively.

"Try it in Hawaiian," she called.

He glared at her. She was teasing him, and in some moment of terrible weakness, like remembering them laughing over that awful painting, he liked it.

She wagged her phone at him and made a great show of looking it up.

"Hele pela," she suggested, trying, without much luck, to swallow a snicker. "It means *get out*. Go away!"

Morgan glared at her, taking in her laughter-filled expression, her teasing tone. The most dangerous thing to do would be to play along.

So, naturally, he played along. He fanned his foot at the chicken, and yelled, *"Hele pela,"* and then the English translation.

The chicken gave him a baleful look, regained its feet with regal calm and strutted toward the edge of the road.

Meg could not hold it back any longer. She was full-out laughing now. He glanced back at her and she looked beautiful, the sun caressing flawless skin, her head thrown back showing him the delicate curve of her tender neck. Her hair was falling out of that clip.

Don't encourage her, he warned himself.

And then he encouraged her by flapping his arms and yelling *"hela pela."*

And then, helpless against it, he found himself laughing, too, as he returned to the cart.

How long since he had laughed? Nothing had seemed funny for a long, long time. And yet, less than ten minutes with his ex beside him, and there it was, a dangerous lightness of spirit.

With renewed concentration, he focused on the road. Meg, wisely, no longer trusted a smooth journey, and tightened her hold on the side posts, which, come to think of it, was a very good strategy for keeping her hands off of him!

Not that she had given any indication she was having trouble keeping her hands off of him.

Unless her cool, soothing touch on his wrist this morning counted.

"What's with the chickens?" she asked him when he had to swerve to miss another one that had darted out on the pathway in front of them.

He liked to think he was a quick learner. He didn't stop this time!

"I read that they've been here since the island was first inhabited, but they were contained. Tropical storms Inika and Iwa in the eighties and nineties destroyed the coops, and they were free to do as they pleased. Which is multiply, apparently. There're very few natural predators to contain them, and endless food sources."

"You always know *everything*," she said, pleased, and he remembered how much *this*—her approval, her admiration—had meant to him.

Just like her gift was seeing things through an artist's eye, this was what he did. He saw things from a business perspective. He enjoyed experiences more if he had the whole picture. He researched. He did his homework. He took in everything, because you could never be sure when knowledge of a certain obscure fact was going to be helpful in making good decisions. In business.

And in life.

Because suddenly obscure facts seemed like a good way to keep the barriers up between Morgan and his ex-wife.

"The sugar industry came here in the 1830s," he told her. "At its height, about a hundred thousand acres of this island were planted in sugar cane. But, just like with the pineapple plantations, successful unionization in the thirties drove industry to seek cheaper labor in other countries. The land value of the fields became greater than its value under cultivation. And then Hurricane Inika—"

"Freer of chickens!"

He smiled at her tone. "Came along and damaged major infrastructure and turned out to be the final blow for an industry already staggering under pressure."

"It's kind of sad that profits came before people just trying to have a better life," she mused.

"Ah, yes, the evil of business."

"Quit being so touchy!"

Tell that to a man who hadn't been left because he was too successful.

An uneasy silence fell between them.

"Oh!" Meg cried. "Stop!"

For a moment, Morgan thought maybe she had had enough of him and his corporate mentality. She could turn on a hair—as her abandonment of their marriage had proven—and maybe she had decided she was going to walk back to the resort rather than spend another minute with him.

But Meg scrambled off the golf cart and took a trail through jungle-like foliage. He saw that, as a passenger, she had seen an easily missed sign promising a waterfall.

It was wrong to feel relieved that she wasn't leaving. Tension between them would be the best possible strategy for getting through the next few days.

Knowing he shouldn't, he could not resist following her. The pathway led up a rise to a picnic shelter roofed in palm fronds. The open-air structure sat beside a tiny pool, with a tiny stream of water trickling over and between moss-covered rocks into it, and then exiting through lush growth out the other side.

"It's so beautiful," she whispered.

"Will you paint it?"

"It feels too big for me," she said, her voice soft.

"If anyone could do it justice, that person is you."

"Thank you for always believing in me," she whispered.

He changed the subject, rapidly!

"Parts of *Jurassic Park* were filmed here. I can see why. It's just a few steps from the paved pathway, but it feels primitive. Pristine. Untouched."

Somehow, trotting out that fact didn't help him keep his barriers up at all. Meg's face was radiant with wonder.

This is what had attracted him to her from the very first. Maybe because she was an artist, she saw beauty in a way others did not.

In fact, Meg did not seem to just *see* it, but to experience it with all her senses, as if she was pulling the beauty down deep inside herself, where she could find it and believe in it, even when life went terribly wrong.

Which hers had done.

And his had done.

The first time he saw her painting *Out of the Ashes*, it had been four years since his brother, his sister-in-law and his niece and nephew had all perished in the fire that had swept through Sarah's Reach on a cold autumn night.

He had known, looking at that painting, that Morgan would be the one who saved him.

But what had she saved him for?

Just to break him again?

Morgan suddenly regretted telling Caylee any-

CARA COLTER 73

thing she needed from him he would give her. Because it was obvious that what Caylee thought she needed was for him and Meg to reunite and live happily ever after so that her own investment in love and the future seemed more certain.

That was why she had thrown them together on this errand.

She thought if she made the clumsy effort to reunite them, nature would take its course. There had always been strong—and very obvious—chemistry between Morgan and Meg.

Caylee would certainly take delight in their current accommodation dilemma, though hopefully that would be sorted out before she even found out about it. He could, unfortunately, see her having a whispered conversation with Keona to make sure that the estranged couple stayed together in Huipu as long as possible.

Morgan had to admit if he was correct that Caylee would like them back together, her strategy of forced proximity was a strong one.

CHAPTER SEVEN

MEG HAD SEEN every one of his losses flash through Morgan's eyes this morning when she had touched his arm. She had assumed he had been to Hawaii before, but she had known instantly that he had been swamped by memories of simpler times at his family's cottage, Sarah's Reach. Though the Hart family had the wealth of the world at their disposal, they had chosen that place over and over again.

He had shared so much about that amazing cottage with her, a story that ended in unthinkable tragedy.

It was one of the things that had drawn them together, initially.

They both understood, completely, what it was to lose a piece of your heart. They had both lost their brothers. But Morgan had lost even more.

In some ways he came from the opposite of her. Her family had been a small, desperate unit: a single mother, her and her brother, Bryan, who had a disability. She did not know who her father was, and had never met her grandparents.

Her memories of childhood were hellish. Poverty. Suffering. What little there was in the family for resources—including love—went to her brother. Meg had found refuge in art. And friendships, particularly her friendship with Caylee, who she had met in the first grade.

Morgan's family, on the other hand, had been prosperous. Boisterous. Large. Tightly knit. They had a history that went back over generations.

It was from him sharing those many memories that Meg had longed for that thing she had never had, and also came to understand just how much family meant to him.

He had never been able to talk about his niece, Kendra, or his nephew, James, without his voice becoming hoarse with emotion.

And at the same time, he had known he honored them—and her—by entrusting her with the stories of his family's love.

If she knew one thing about Morgan, she knew this. The thing he wanted most was to be part of that again—that wonderful, messy, chaotic unit called family—that a freak fire had taken from his life.

In one night, his brother, Logan, gone. His sister-in-law, Amelia. His niece. His nephew.

He was supposed to have been there at the family cottage that weekend. At the last minute he'd had to cancel.

And so he had lived. But his mother and father had never been the same. His mother had died—he said—of a broken heart within a year of the accident. His father, reeling from too many losses, had withered away, until he, too, was gone.

And so Morgan—terrified of love, and longing for it at the same time—had entrusted his battered heart to Meg.

And she had thought she would be worthy of it.

That they would build a family together.

That something beautiful could come out of the ashes, just as a painting she had done before her body knew him—but her spirit already did—had promised.

But then she had sat in the doctor's office and listened to his devastating words.

You won't ever be able to have a baby.

The one thing that Morgan needed, wanted, cried for in his sleep, she could not give him. She could not give him the family, a baby, the final ingredient that she knew would fuse the broken pieces of his heart together, and make it even stronger than it had been before.

She had known she had to leave him, to give

him the gift of the only destiny that would bring him back fully from the abyss.

In a life that had required both great love and great sacrifice from her—Bryan had always come first in the family dynamic—leaving Morgan had been the greatest act of love and sacrifice that had ever been asked of her.

But here she was, in this enchanted place, with Morgan beside her, walking the tightrope between loving him enough to let him go, and enjoying this time with him as if it was a gift from the universe.

It would be way too easy to lean into his words that she was worthy of painting this incredible landscape.

He had always believed in her so unconditionally.

In fact, she was pretty sure most of her success as an artist came when he had purchased *Out of the Ashes* and made it the official art of the foundation that honored that family he had lost to the fire.

She had never asked herself if she would have been as successful without his endorsement.

Without his love.

Because those things had always had a meant-to-be feeling to them, her destiny and his as intertwined as a braided rope of sweetgrass.

The only thing that didn't have a meant-to-be

feeling was her decision to leave, to do what love did, and put his needs ahead of her own.

"Hey," Morgan said gently. "Come back."

His fingers were resting lightly on her cheek, and when she looked up into his eyes, he was regarding her intensely, as if her thoughts were an open book to him.

He had always been able to read her way too accurately, and she ducked out from under his fingertips, even as she wanted to cover them with her own hand and draw them to her lips.

"Last one to the cart is a rotten egg," she called.

With a shout, he raced by her and slid into the driver's seat. "I win," he said when she joined him, breathless. "You know what I want for a prize?"

A kiss, her heart answered way too hopefully.

"No more chicken references."

She should have been relieved that his mind was not going down the same track as hers, but she felt anything but.

"I'm egg-static that I didn't agree to a prize," she said.

"Don't crow about it," he shot back.

"Ha. You're out of cluck."

"You're ruffling my feathers."

It had always been like this between them, these easy interchanges, feeding off similar senses of humor and each other's energy.

"Oh, cry me a cackle."

And then the worst possible thing—or maybe the best possible thing—happened. They were both laughing together as if eight months of pure torment were not sitting over them like dark storm clouds.

They pulled into the old plantation village, a small collection of lovely pastel-colored cottages with hip roofs, shady verandas, tidy yards. In one of those yards, a hammock swung gently between two palm trees. Meg was so taken with the serenity of it, she pulled out her phone and took a picture.

"Possible future painting?" Morgan asked.

"Yes." That feeling of being *known* filled Meg with a longing she needed to quash. She focused instead on the enchantment of the commercial center.

There was actually a parking area designated for the golf carts, and they left their vehicle there and walked the few steps to the shopping area. It felt weird and wrong not to be holding his hand, particularly after that feeling of being known.

Morgan must have felt that, too, because he thrust his hands into his shorts pockets, as if to avoid temptation.

Sitting in the shade of towering palms was a town-like atmosphere, with shops lining both sides of a cobblestone street that had long since

been closed to vehicular traffic. The stores, connected by a wooden boardwalk, were a delight
of old clapboard storefronts, some with covered
front verandas. There were open-air cafés and
coffee bars, and the scent of coffee and fresh
baking was in the air. Flowers spilled out of con-
tainers. The colorful chickens strutting about
only added to the ambience.

The shops were just opening, and people were
putting out sandwich boards and display racks.
In front of the cafés and coffee bars, tables and
chairs were being arranged.

"Look." Meg pointed at where a woman was
putting out racks of women's clothing under a
colorful sign that said *Wow-ee Wahine*.

As they made their way toward the boutique,
the cheerful bustle of the morning was suddenly
interrupted.

Protestors came, shoulder to shoulder, down
the street, caring flags and placards and shouting slogans.

Morgan pulled Meg behind him in an instinc-
tive gesture that was very protective. Meg felt
extremely irritated that the protestors were in-
serting themselves and their viewpoints into
such an idyllic setting.

She could tell, by glancing at the firm line of
Morgan's mouth, that he felt the same way.

The storekeeper who had been putting out the display racks paused and glanced at the protestors.

When she turned to Meg and Morgan, her expression was soft.

"So much anger," she said with a gentle shake of her head. "I hope they stay here awhile, so they can understand *aloha*."

Meg felt her irritation melt away, and looked at Morgan. She could tell the woman's words and her lovely, peaceful way of being had had the very same effect on him.

The woman now turned her full, beautiful energy on them.

"Oh!" she said. "I have exactly the right dress for you!"

"I'm not exactly shopping just for myself," Meg told her.

"On your honeymoon?" she asked.

Unfortunately, memories of her honeymoon blasted through her, and Meg could feel herself blushing. She glanced at Morgan. He was looking at his feet.

"Oh, no!" The woman moved toward her and lifted her hand. "You've lost your ring."

Meg was suddenly aware of the white band of skin on her finger where her ring had been. She had never taken it off until a few days ago.

Her eyes skittered to Morgan's ring finger. It,

of course, did not have the telltale band of white of the freshly separated.

He was looking at her finger oddly.

She snatched her hand away and changed the subject.

"No," she said firmly, "we are not on a honeymoon."

The woman looked between them as if their whole history was laid bare to her soft brown eyes.

"We're visiting Kauai for the wedding of friends," Meg explained hastily, then outlined the dilemma of the missing wedding clothes.

"What a wonderful thing to help with!" the shop owner exclaimed. "Come in. Come in. My name's Kamelei. Everything in my shop is designed and made in Hawaii."

Megan watched as Morgan took a glance inside the shop and tried not to look too horrified at the *all things feminine* theme. The crowded little store proudly displayed everything from bras and panties to negligees.

"I'll just go see what I can find for the groomsmen," he said.

"No," Kamelei ordered him. "Sit, sit. You can take the chair on the front lanai. She'll come show you. You'll need to send pictures to the bride. It's her choice."

Meg was glad Kamelei was there to help her

stay focused, because she was distracted by one of the dresses on display.

"The print on this fabric!" she exclaimed, taking a closer look at an exquisite pattern of palm trees, chickens, mountains. "All of Kauai has been captured here."

"I work with local artists, and have their work printed onto fabric. Too busy for the bridesmaid dresses," Kamelei decided with a tilt of her head. She took Meg by the elbow and ushered her into a little curtained alcove at the back of the store, "I'll find everything I have in white."

Moments later, four white sundresses were slipped in through the curtain.

None of them was suited for a bra! Was she really going to model these for Morgan, braless?

Meg drew in a deep breath. This wasn't for her. And it wasn't for Morgan. It was for Caylee, and she needed to suck it up and do whatever needed to be done.

She put on the first dress.

It had been adorable on the hanger, and it was even more so on. The dress had a full skirt, puffy short sleeves and it left a whole lot of leg and cleavage on display.

She stepped self-consciously out of the change cubicle. "I don't think—"

"That's for your friend to decide," Kamelei

said firmly, and shooed her out the door. "Show him. Send photos to the bride."

Meg trudged out the door.

"First one," she announced. Morgan was sitting in a deep wicker chair looking at his phone. It seemed unfair that he had the better of the two jobs.

He looked up.

Something so hot went through his eyes, she felt singed by it.

"Take a picture," she said through tight lips.

He raised his phone, then lowered it. "Do you have to look as if you're going to the gallows?"

She smiled. It felt as if her lips were stretching uncomfortably over her teeth.

"That's worse."

She tried widening the smile.

"Now you're trying too hard."

"Take the damn picture."

"You know, for the world's most gorgeous woman, you're amazingly unphotogenic when you want to be."

Her husband thought she was the world's most gorgeous woman. The longing to be what they had once been nearly swamped her. She needed to focus on the critical part.

"Thank you," she said sarcastically.

"Just try to make it about showing the dress

off, not like you're a prisoner in a flour sack having your mug shot taken."

But a *gorgeous* one, she wanted to remind him. Instead, Meg glared at him. "You know I've always been awkward about having my picture taken."

He sighed. "I'm trying to get the dress to best advantage. Try resting your hand on your hip."

A bit reluctantly, she followed his suggestion.

"And maybe just put your other hand on that post, and put one leg down on the stairs."

"What are you? Mr. Professional Photographer?" she snapped.

"You never know what I might be called to do if planes don't start showing up," he told her mildly. He frowned. "Could you do something with your lips?"

"What does that have to do with showing Caylee the dress?"

He ignored that question. "You know, that thing girls do when they're taking selfies?"

"I don't know," she said stubbornly, even though that was a lie. Though she rarely took selfies of herself, she seemed to be about the only one in the world who did not.

It occurred to her Morgan was enjoying her discomfort very much!

"Do that little pursing thing with your lips, you know, like you're about to use a straw."

Since she didn't want to increase his enjoyment of her discomfort, she went along without complaint. She did as he asked, only she highly exaggerated the pucker of her lips, as if she was leaning forward to kiss a baby. Just as he went to take the picture, she crossed her eyes.

"Nice," he said, looking at the image he had captured with pretend annoyance. He snapped his fingers. "Think of your happiest moment."

That was easy. And also, heartbreakingly hard.

I do.

It had been the best moment of Meg's entire life, looking into Morgan's face, and being sure she saw forever.

Unless you counted what followed, his cool lips and her heated skin, the sense of owning each other in the most sacred of ways…

CHAPTER EIGHT

"THERE," MORGAN SAID with satisfaction, clicking the picture. "Meg, you finally look like you."

"I don't see how looking like me has anything to do with showing Caylee the dress," Meg complained.

"You finally lowered your shoulders from around your ears, that's how. Why are you so self-conscious about having your picture taken?"

Even though she had said that herself, she didn't want to admit the truth. Maybe it wasn't about having her picture taken! Maybe it was about modeling for her husband. She turned to go try on the next dress.

"Don't go yet. I'll send this to Caylee. Hopefully, she loves it and…oh, that was fast," Morgan said when his phone pinged. For a moment he looked hopeful and then his face fell. So, despite tormenting Meg by making her pose for the camera, he wasn't loving this exercise any more than she was.

"She loves the dress, but it's a definite no."

Meg went back to the changeroom. The next white dress was a tube style, sleeveless and slinky. It required a great deal of wriggling to get into it. It was an obvious no, but when she slipped out of the change room with it on, Kamelei pinned a square of white lace to her hair and thrust a bouquet of flowers into her hands.

"There," she said with satisfaction, turning Meg toward the mirror.

The dress was way too revealing. It looked as if it was painted on. Meg did not want to model it for Morgan, but again, she sucked it up, telling herself it was for the greater good.

As she came out the door, she saw a little boy had appeared on the lanai. He was holding a chicken, and Morgan was leaning over in his chair, his hand out, making a clucking sound way in the back of his throat.

The little boy was laughing and so was Morgan. Probably because of his niece and nephew, Morgan had an ease around children that few men had.

When Meg saw the light in his face as he interacted with the little boy, it felt as if the wisdom of her decision was confirmed.

But she needed to quit being distracted and find out if Marjorie was going to be the one who would give Morgan the life he deserved.

"I can't believe this," Meg said, charmed despite herself. "I leave for one second, and you're romancing a chicken!"

"It's not any old chicken," he said. "It's Henry."

The little boy shouted with laughter. "I'm Henry," he said. "This is Clyde."

Meg saw that Morgan's mistake had been intentional to make the little boy laugh.

"Come meet him," he said, and she came over and shifted the flowers to one hand. But when she tentatively reached out, the chicken squawked, flapped its wings and ruffled its feathers.

She took a startled step back, and Morgan, by second nature, reached out and steadied her, his hand on her wrist.

Henry tucked Clyde under his arm and left the lanai on the run.

Morgan released her arm, almost as if he hadn't realized he had taken it, and watched the child and the chicken depart with an unguarded smile.

"You can always tell," she told him softly.

"Tell what?" he asked gruffly, to hide the fact he was embarrassed she had witnessed his softer side. Not that his softer side was any mystery to her. On the other hand, in his mind, she had betrayed his trust. No wonder he wanted to hide the vulnerable parts of himself from her.

"If people like children."

"I guess you can," he said, but his tone suggested *who cares if they do or don't.*

Well, she didn't care if most people did or didn't. Only someone he was romantically involved with. And she didn't know how to probe that without seeming way too interested in his private life.

Meg became aware of something creeping through all her focus on Morgan. Seeing him with that little boy had brought back every feeling of that day she had been in the doctor's office and heard the news.

She thought she had dealt with her sense of loss and grief, but now, seeing that little boy, she felt it anew.

She would never have a chubby little boy calling her Mommy, looking at her with dancing, dark eyes like his father's, holding out a rock or a dandelion or a frog, inviting her to rediscover the entire world through his innocent eyes.

She would never have a little girl, with curly, sandy locks just like Morgan's, tongue caught between teeth as she labored over a drawing, or giggled and tossed handfuls of bubbles over her head at bath time.

Meg could feel herself being drawn further down the road of grief: no warm little bodies snuggled into her for stories before bed, no first day of kindergarten, no cold spring days at T-ball practice, no wiping away tears and dispensing of healing hugs and kisses—

"Meg?"

She started and looked at Morgan, who was frowning at her.

"Is something wrong?" he asked.

She jerked herself back to the here and now, and forced a smile. He did not look convinced, and so she did a little twirl in the dress. When she faced him again, she could see her distraction had worked.

Morgan was now intensely focused on the dress. His dark brown eyes darkened until they looked black. His mouth fell open.

"Holy," he croaked.

He quickly lifted his phone and hid behind it. He didn't give any instructions this time about Meg thinking happy thoughts.

Still, she left her sadness behind her and contemplated how evil it was that it was her turn to enjoy his discomfort, and she planned to play it to the absolute max!

Morgan really hoped Meg would go and take that dress off soon. It was crazy sexy, something suitable for a late night at a club, not for a wedding dress, not even as the emergency stand-in model. The little posy of flowers she was carrying, and the veil pinned in her hair, did nothing to water down the message of the dress.

"I'm pretty sure that veil has more fabric in it

than the dress," he told her. He hoped the croak was gone from his voice, but he didn't think he was that good an actor.

Of course, *now* Meg found her inner model. She pulled the little scrap of lace in front of her face, and blinked at him from behind it. She walked across the lanai toward him. He wasn't sure if she was deliberately swishing her hips like that, or if the dress just made it seem that way. The hem was slithering up the length of her legs.

Once a man had known a woman as his wife, in every sense of that word, was it ever possible to put *that* behind you? He knew the tang of perspiration on her skin, and he knew the mole that was hidden where no one else had ever seen it, and he knew the location of a secret dimple...

"She says no," he cried when his phone pinged.

Meg gave him a knowing smile, before she turned and sashayed away. She threw a glance over her shoulder, her look filtered by the veil. He wished he would have been looking anywhere but at her butt, checking out if the clingy dress revealed the secret dimple. It did.

The next dress she came out in, thankfully, was demure. It was a simple white sleeveless knee-length sheath, overlaid with lace.

Morgan knew Caylee would say yes.

Meg looked like a bride.

So much so that he felt the sharp knife-edge of regret pierce him. Would things have gone differently if she had had *this*?

This moment in her white dress, with a veil in her hair, carrying flowers?

They hadn't been dating all that long before Morgan had known she was the one. He'd also known, shocked at his own old-fashionedness, that as glorious as their lovemaking was, he would never feel right about it until he married her.

Because she was that kind of girl. The forever kind.

And she drew out that kind of man in him.

The man who wanted to live up to what he saw shining in her eyes when she looked at him.

She believed in his decency. His honor.

Still, there had been no white dress, no cathedral filled with guests, no amazing dinner after, no first dance.

A man who had failed at his marriage wondered, endlessly, what could have fixed it.

Any of those things? The wedding of her dreams, like the one that Caylee and Jonathon were putting together on this enchanted isle?

But no, he'd been selfish. The last gathering of his family had been at the funeral—his brother, his sister-in-law, his niece, his nephew in polished caskets going up the aisle. His mother had collapsed, and his father had tried so heartbreakingly hard to be strong.

And Morgan could not do it.

He could not gather with family without those memories coming up. He could not have a traditional wedding without his brother at his side, without Kendra skipping down the aisle tossing flower petals, without James taking tiny steps, his tongue stuck out between his teeth, his eyes fastened, anxious, on the pillow that carried the ring he'd been entrusted with.

Meg didn't have any family to speak of. Her brother, like his, was dead. Her mother was a mess of addiction and treatment, and addiction again.

He thought that was why Meg had gotten his wish not to have a large celebration so completely. He thought it had suited her perfectly, too.

But had it really?

His phone pinged, and he glanced at it, relieved to take his eyes off Meg.

"Caylee says that's the one," he said with relief. He was not sure how many more wedding dresses he could stand having modeled by Meg, who had never had one. Should he ask her if she regretted that? Somehow it seemed like a topic he could not broach.

Once upon a time—back when he still believed in *once upon a time*—there was no topic he could not broach with Meg.

"I'm hungry," he announced, and he was. Hungry for the way things used to be. No food could ever fill that—though he was willing to give it a try.

"You just had a huge breakfast."

He glanced at his watch. "Hours ago. The chicken turned my thoughts to food."

"That chicken was a pet!"

"I can't help myself."

"Well, then you'll be thinking of food a lot here on Kauai," she told him. "We're not done. Not even close. We have to choose bridesmaid dresses, and something for the groomsmen."

He talked her into eating something first. He gave Kamelei the mission of finding some suitable bridesmaid dresses for when they returned.

"If you want an authentic Hawaiian experience, get the *musubi* from the food truck on the corner," she called after them.

"I'm all for the authentic Hawaiian experience," Meg claimed, but she wasn't so sure when she stood in front of a dilapidated truck with a banner that proclaimed it Kauai's Purveyor of Fine Food.

She was stunned to see what the recommended *musubi* was made out of!

"How can Spam be Hawaiian?" she asked doubtfully. Since the purveyor himself—wearing a name tag that said Tim and a T-shirt that claimed Spam was not just something in your inbox—was leaning eagerly over his counter toward them, she didn't add what she was obviously thinking. As was Morgan.

How could highly processed ground pork that came in a tin with a peel-back lid be considered fine food?

"It came to the Hawaiian Islands during the Second World War," Tim told them. "We've been having a love affair with it ever since. You can even get Spam-flavored potato chips at the grocery store here."

"Oh," she said weakly.

"Can't wait to try those," Morgan said. She shot him a look. She was pretty sure he was serious!

"The *musubi* was recommended," Morgan said.

"Virgins?" their host asked them.

Morgan slid Meg a look. She was blushing.

"I mean *musubi* virgins," Tim clarified cheerfully. "I mean it's obvious you two are—"

Tim didn't finish the sentence, just wagged his eyebrows wickedly.

Geez. How annoying that something so untrue seemed obvious to complete strangers.

Meg giggled uneasily. "I think I'll have the fresh fruit platter."

"We'll take two *musubi*," Morgan said firmly.

He led her to a picnic table.

"I'm not eating pan-fried Spam—in oyster sauce—wrapped in roasted nori seaweed," she whispered to him.

"Don't forget the sushi rice," he reminded her.

Their host came and put the plates down in front of them. He'd either forgotten the fruit or didn't want it to dilute the full *musubi* experience. Tim waited, smiling. It became a contest of who could outwait whom.

Apparently the purveyor of Kauai's finest did not have the urgency of the fate of outfitting an entire wedding party in a few hours riding on his shoulders. Tim had all day.

Realizing she was not going to be able to outwait him, Meg reluctantly picked up the *musubi*, which looked like an extra fat sushi roll.

Morgan watched, amused as Meg closed her eyes, looked as if she was saying a prayer and then took a delicate bite. Her eyes opened. They widened.

"Morgan," she breathed, "you are not going to believe this."

Their host bowed and left them.

Morgan bit into pure ambrosia, and felt oddly grateful for one more moment like this with her.

The magic of pure discovery.

When they returned to Wow-ee Wahine, Kamelei had chosen a selection of sundresses she thought would be perfect for the bridal party. She had hung them outside in the window casings. Meg took pictures and sent them while chatting with Caylee.

"I think this one would be best in the photos," Meg advised her friend. "The deep burgundy won't compete with the backdrop, and there's no pattern."

"They have four, in the sizes we need?"

Kamelei nodded.

"Take them. Done and done," Caylee decided with obvious relief. Morgan was relieved, too, since she hadn't even asked Meg to try the dresses on. He wasn't sure he was up to another modeling session.

Since plastic bags were banned in Hawaii, Kamelei carefully wrapped the bridesmaid dresses together in brown paper and gave it to them with the other dress, which had already been wrapped.

"You can return them if you don't end up needing them," Kamelei said.

And there it was. *Aloha.* Concern for the wedding—and the well-being—of complete strangers overriding the sale.

She pointed them in the direction of the only men's store in the mall. It was called Surf Bums, and it had a selection of casual beachwear that lived up to its name. After endless going back and forth with Caylee, they finally had a backup plan for the guys' side of the wedding party.

Plain white T-shirts and the most subdued board shorts in stock, which were black with a faint palm tree pattern on them.

It was now late afternoon and Meg and Morgan were hot, sticky and tired.

"Let's have a cold drink before we go back," he suggested.

They found a café and settled on the lanai at a wooden table under a bright awning. A man strummed a ukulele on a small stage. Morgan ordered a light beer, and Meg had a slushy made with Kauai's famous Sugarloaf White pineapple.

The drink had the unfortunate name of Pining For You.

"It's delicious," she said, and closed her cute little mouth over the straw, just like she'd done earlier for the pictures. "Want to try?"

No, he didn't want to try it! His lips closing over the same straw her lips had closed over seemed way too intimate. Which was ridiculous. If he refused, she would know he was being ridiculous.

"Sure," he said.

She passed him the drink and he took a sip. He'd been right. Way too intimate. He passed it back, irritated that the drink had an extra sweetness, as if the morning with Meg had made all of him come alive, even his taste buds. Even such a simple thing—sharing a drink on a beautiful afternoon—suddenly felt rife with complication.

Still, it was hard to remain irritated when it was idyllic sitting in the shade, watching the chickens and the tourists flock through the shops.

Then a man with a gourd drum joined the man with the ukulele, and a woman joined them. She was slender and golden-skinned, her shiny black hair—crowned with a leaf-and-flower headdress—cascaded down past the middle of her back. She had a lei around her neck, a chest covering that appeared to be made of coconut shells and a ti-leaf skirt.

As the man strummed the ukulele, the drum put out a pulsing beat. The dancer's graceful, sinuous movements were explained as she performed traditional hula, a storytelling dance of the Hawaiian Islands.

More and more people gathered to watch the performance. Morgan cast a glance at Meg. She was enchanted. The sense of discovering a new world with her intensified, though the world the hula dancer was opening up was soft and sensual, probably not the best thing to be experiencing with your nearly ex-wife.

He switched to water after the first beer. He did not want his guard coming down right now, but Meg ordered a second slushy.

She had nearly finished it when the dancer pointed at her. "Come try," she called.

Normally, Meg would not be the kind of person who was up for audience-participation invitations.

But she obviously could not think of a way to gracefully refuse. So, she lifted her eyebrows at him, left her chair and joined the dancer on the stage. She was asked to kick off her shoes.

"I'm going to teach you the very basic first step of hula," the dancer said. "It's called *kalakaua*. Mirror what I do."

The women faced each other. The dancer put her elbows up, hands pointed toward each other, fingertips just about touching at her chest level. Then she sank, slowly, bending her knees. To the exact beat of the drum, she turned to the audience and thrust one hip with a sinuous grace. She turned the other direction and thrust the other hip. She alternated her arms as she did this.

Meg gamely followed her lead, and they did the movement a dozen or so times.

The teacher nodded her approval. "All right, we are ready for double *kalakaua*."

The beat of the music intensified. Now, the women turned to the audience and moved one hip forward, and then the other, before turning and doing it on the other side.

It was a simple movement, so stunningly sensual it took Morgan's breath away. He was entranced as Meg, normally somewhat inhibited, gave herself over to the impromptu dance lesson.

Meg was a little awkward, but only at first. Though she had never been any kind of athlete—he remembered trying to teach her how to throw a Frisbee—she soon caught on that she just needed to mirror what the other woman was doing.

He watched the exact moment that she let go, and gave herself over to the experience, her body surrendering to the music. He wasn't sure how much of the inhibition was a part of her he had never really seen before, and how much was the fault of the slushy.

As Meg mastered one step, the teacher would move on. "You're a natural," she said, and the audience applauded their agreement. Meg, normally on the shy side, was soaking it up.

Morgan looked around, feeling as if he might have to go to war if some lecherous old men were eyeing up his wife.

Nearly not his wife, he reminded himself sternly.

The two women looked absolutely stunning as they performed the dance in perfect sync, arms moving as gently as the breeze, bodies swaying, hips moving.

Meg's eyes locked with his. She moved her hips, her bare stomach swiveled, her arms floated out from her body. He had a sudden sense of being alone with her, as if she was dancing this dance only for him. As if it was an invitation.

To know her.

Of course, he already did know her in that way, but he was shocked by the erotic nature of this experience, and how he felt as much like Meg's husband as he ever had.

The drum beat died away. The women became still, and then the teacher hugged Meg.

"You were awesome," she told her, and the audience agreed with thunderous applause. Meg blushed and curtsied to the audience. She carried her shoes back to the table and sat down, her face alight, though she wouldn't meet his eyes as she finished the drink in one long slurp.

Another slushy appeared in front of her.

"Compliments of that gentleman over there," the waitress said.

Morgan glared *over there*. It wasn't even a lecherous old man. A lecherous young man, grinning cheekily at Meg. Handsome, too.

Good grief, was he jealous?

Of course he was jealous! He just couldn't ever let her—the woman who had dumped him—know that!

The dancer was joined by several other dancers onstage. They announced they would perform, as their last number, the Tahitian *ote'a.*

The performance was quite incredible, the drumming fast-paced, the dancers keeping up with it with astonishing hip rotations. Meg was rapt.

"Wow," she breathed. "I'm glad I didn't get asked to do that one."

Me too, Morgan thought.

"Very common to have an afternoon sprinkle in the tropics," the ukulele player announced as the women finished their performance. "That's why it's so lush here. You might want an umbrella."

Morgan looked at the sky. There was no sign of rain.

Megan looked at her empty slushy glass, a bit bewildered.

"I think I'm tipsy," she whispered, mortified. "Did that have alcohol in it?"

"I thought you probably assumed that."

"I didn't! Why didn't you tell me?" she demanded.

"I thought you knew. Couldn't you taste it?"

"All I could taste was the pineapple. And maybe some coconut. Like a piña colada."

"An alcoholic drink," he pointed out.

She narrowed her eyes at him, as if he had known and she didn't.

She made her way back to the golf cart, her slight tipsiness made unfortunately hilarious by the fact she was trying to act as if she was completely sober. The graceful dancer of half an hour ago was completely vanquished, Morgan noted with relief.

He got her seated and the packages safely stowed behind them, and then took the driver's seat.

Halfway back, black clouds boiled up over the mountains. But if this was a "sprinkle," Morgan didn't want to see what a storm would look like. In the blink of an eye, a beautiful day turned into a tropical deluge.

Water fell from the sky in sheets. It sounded like drums as it pounded the foliage around them.

He was a Vancouver boy, born and raised. Morgan thought he knew every single thing there was to know about rain.

And he was wrong.

He was one hundred percent wrong.

CHAPTER NINE

"I'VE NEVER SEEN rain like this, ever," Meg said, her voice slightly slurred, but nevertheless awed.

Morgan hadn't either. The paved pathway was turning into a stream, the water pulling at the wheels of the cart.

The canvas roof of the cart began to sag, and then it dripped. Even without the failure of the roof, they would have been getting wet as the rain slashed into the cart sideways. They were completely soaked in seconds.

"The clothes are going to be ruined," Meg wailed, and then yanked the packages out of the back—nearly falling out of the cart to do so—before trying to fold her body over them to protect them.

Even for all the trouble they'd gone through to get those clothes, it was probably a measure of her altered state that Meg thought they should be a priority right now. He could barely see the track in front of them, and he was using all his strength to maintain control of the steering wheel. He was pretty sure their cart was about to turn into a boat, and he was not sure if it could float.

"Is everything okay?" Meg asked, her eyes suddenly fastened on his face.

The words *flash flood* were going through his brain, but he deliberately kept his tone calm.

"Oh, yeah," he said, "just a little tropical squall."

They might be barreling toward a divorce, but he felt one hundred percent like her husband in that moment.

This was what he had signed up for when he said *I do*.

This had felt like what he was born to do.

Protect her. Keep her safe.

In that moment, with the water beginning to boil under the cart, he was aware signing a piece of paper was never going to change that.

Meg gasped. "What is happening?"

We're getting swept away.

"The water was just pooling on that part of the road."

That was not exactly true. He glanced over his shoulder when he heard a roaring sound like a jet getting ready to take off. A torrent of water, just a few yards from where they had just been, rolled over the road, dark with mud and debris.

Meg turned back toward the roar and stared. When she looked back at him, she looked suddenly very sober.

What he saw in her eyes, though, was not terror. It was complete trust in him. Even as he vowed to be worthy of it, the earth seemed to be trembling under the cart. He saw the reason. Another torrent of water was racing toward the path in front of them.

To his enormous relief, Morgan realized they were at the picnic area they had visited briefly this morning. He remembered it was on a rise.

With all his strength he wrested the cart off the path. He got out. The water was swirling around his knees, the current unbelievable powerful.

Hanging on to the frame, he made his way around to her side.

"Leave the parcels," he ordered her.

She gave him a look as if he'd lost his mind, and hugged them tighter to herself. He yanked her out of the cart and tossed her over his shoulder. In a few steps, his feet mercifully found dry ground. Well, not dry, but not submerged in two feet of water, either.

Carefully, he set Meg down.

She was still clutching the packages. She turned back the way they had come and watched as the water scooped up the cart and it floated several feet before it lodged on high ground again.

She looked like a drowned rat. He hadn't realized she was wearing makeup until he saw it was smudged under her eyes. Her hair was plastered to her skull, and her clothes were plastered to her curves. Rain ran down her face in rivulets.

She had never looked quite so beautiful.

Or had the hula dancer just heightened his awareness of the sensual? The hula dancer, the unexpected storm, the close call with calamity.

"It's my curse," she wailed.

"That's ridiculous," he told her firmly. "No one's in the hospital."

"Yet," she said bleakly.

"Come on, the shelter is right over here."

She stumbled—way too much white pineapple slushy—and he grabbed her hand, and half pulled, half carried her toward the shelter.

It was open-air, but the picnic table in the middle of it was dry and protected. Three chickens were roosting underneath of it. The rain hammered on the palm-frond roof and the wind swept in.

Even though it was not cold at all, as he watched when Meg turned back and looked at the river now gushing down the paved trail, she began to shake.

Her soaked shorts and top were clinging to her, every bit as revealing as that second slinky dress had been. She looked as sensual as the hula dancer had been.

Morgan felt a tingling across the back of his

neck, an awareness that one danger had been replaced with another.

Confirming this, Meg *finally* set down the packages, but only to press her soaked, trembling body against his own wetness.

Give me strength, Morgan thought, and tried to step away from her. Instead, her hands, frantic, wrapped around his neck. And then she was pulling his lips to her lips.

"Hey," he said gruffly, managing to get his lips away, though her hold around his neck tightened, "you've had a little too much to drink and—"

Her lips took his.

She's drunk, he told himself. *Don't do it.*

But she ran the tip of her tongue over the edge of his upper lip in that way that she knew drove him mad.

This had been brewing between them all day, an awareness growing, just out of sight, but as certainly as this invisible storm had been gathering strength in those high valleys hidden behind jagged mountain peaks.

Now, competing with all the sounds of the storm, was a voice, just as insistent, inside of Morgan.

And it said, *Why not?*

Why not give himself into the kind of forces of nature that swept things away without warning? Maybe especially a man's ability to say no.

Wasn't a man's idea that he was in control the worst illusion of all?

They were still married. He had just figured out in some way, no matter if they made their divorce official or not, he was always going to feel married to Meg.

As if it was his job to protect her and keep her safe, forever.

Or maybe he was just making excuses for the fact he was already one hundred percent certain that he was not a big enough man to stand up to the temptation of what she was offering, no matter how dishonorable that might be.

And, come to that, where had being the decent, honorable guy gotten him last time?

And come to that, she was an adult woman, completely capable of making decisions without him. She'd proven that by leaving him, hadn't she?

Meg was not drunk. Not anymore. She hadn't been drunk, anyway. Tipsy at best. No, there was something else running through her.

Pure adrenaline.

And primal awareness that life was short.

That in a blink—*Mrs. Hart, I'm sorry to tell you this*—the whole life she had planned could be snatched away from her.

She had, somehow, evaded the curse, and a relieved euphoria was sweeping through her, obliterating her rational thought, just as the water and mud had obliterated the path behind them.

She could not keep her hands or her lips off her ex-husband. She never had been able to. Being with him all day, modeling for him, discovering new things, the drinks, the hula dancer, the storm—maybe even the chickens chortling away under the table—all seemed to be encouraging her to grab life while she could. Even the pungent smell rising from the earth seemed to call to her to explore the deep mysteries of primal urges, or creation itself.

Of course, she was going to regret this later. Terribly.

All those months of making herself not call him, making herself not beg him, making herself not throw herself at his feet and explain it to him…all that agony of discipline out the window, those efforts as temporary and as insubstantial as the mist and mountain cloud that pressed in on them from all sides.

Right now, for Meg, later did not matter. In fact, it was incomprehensible.

All that mattered was the bliss of Morgan's arms around her, the heat of his wet, strong, familiar body pressed full along the length of hers. All that mattered was the familiar taste of his lips on her tongue. All that mattered was the moment when, with a strangled groan, he surrendered and wrapped his hands through the wet tangle of her hair and kissed her back.

Ferociously.

Hungrily.

Honestly.

They were in Hawaii. They were in a public place. How could something so wrong feel so right?

Even the chickens seemed to know that chances of anyone else being out in the storm were slender to none. Meg had watched the road close behind them. It was probably also now impassable in front of them.

They were utterly and completely alone in this place that paid complete homage to mystical forces that could not and would not be tamed by something so small, so fragile, as human will.

CHAPTER TEN

MEG WAS AWARE her hand—no, her entire body—
was trembling, not from cold, but from white-
hot desire. The shaking was so pronounced she
was having trouble slipping the buttons free on
Morgan's shirt. It felt like sweet torture, forcing
them, one by one, through holes that seemed to
have shrunk with the rain.

Once she had dispensed with the buttons, she
worked on peeling the sodden fabric away from
his belly and chest. Finally, she saw what she
had longed for ever since she had glimpsed him
lying in bed, naked, last night.

With hungry eyes, Meg took in the beautiful
expanse of his flawless skin stretched over the
broad plains of his chest and the taut drum of
his belly.

She touched it. She thought, because he was so
wet, Morgan's skin would be cold. But it wasn't.
It radiated heat and felt like silk. Letting her fingertips explore him made her so aware of how

acutely incomplete she had felt without *this* in her life.

But soon, touching him with her fingertips was not enough to quell the need, a tiny flame within her that demanded to be fed. Meg kissed his chest. She flicked the hard pebble of his nipple with the tip of her tongue.

Combustion. The spark flickered stronger, took hold, licked heat into parts of her that had been cold for way too long.

The growing flame fanned between them, touching, drawing back, touching again, stronger, hotter.

Morgan's groan was raw and his fingers found her blouse. He undid the knot at her waist with an easy flick of his wrist, dispensed with the buttons, drew the fabric over her shoulders and off her arms with the ease with which one might peel a banana.

And then he shrugged off his own wet shirt, and the sodden clothing lay in a puddle at their feet.

Only the filmy fabric of her bra was preventing them being skin on skin, and with his eyes never leaving her face, Morgan dispensed with that, too.

And then lowered his head over what had been revealed.

"You are so beautiful," he whispered, his voice

raw, and then his lips, hot, found her breast, and she drew his head closer against her, reveling in the sweet torment of sensation.

He dropped his head lower, trailing his tongue down the center line of her body, flicking it in and out of her belly button.

Her shorts—and then his—joined the clothes at their feet. The moist, warm air embraced them, their skin pebbled with droplets of humidity, perspiration, need.

There hadn't been a volcanic eruption on Kauai for four hundred thousand years, but it felt as if the rain all around them had turned to fire as he poured his white-hot kisses down on her, slowly anointing every inch of her skin, cherishing every single thing about her that made her a woman.

She gasped and tangled her hands in his hair when Morgan dropped on his knees before her and wrapped his arms around the small of her back, taking her as a willing captive.

He dropped a trail of fire—exquisitely possessive, tender—as he moved downward. Without a trace of self-consciousness, he tasted her most secret of places, then kissed her inner thighs with deep reverence.

When he released her, and stood up, Meg was

quivering with sensation, and the same need to *know* him that he had just shown to her.

She worshipped the strong lines of his magnificent male body with her eyes, and then with her lips, and then with her tongue.

There was not one part of him that was not entirely beautiful, there was not one part of him that she did not come to know completely. She *loved* his need of her, his trembling, the sounds that came from him as he exercised exquisite discipline, waiting for her to feel complete in her exploration of him.

She rose, once again, and pressed against him, swaying and sliding, until he uttered a muted groan of complete surrender.

She whispered *yes* to that, marveled at the powerful beauty of a man and a woman coming to this complete understanding of what it was for the masculine and the feminine to dance together.

With gentle, exquisite strength, Morgan turned her, then lifted her onto the edge of the picnic table. He scanned her face, a question in his eyes. Her truth met that question, and her legs wrapped around the small of his back.

His lips took hers, not with gentle welcome now, but fiercely, possessively, urgently. The firestorm was not just outside of them, but infusing every cell of their beings, burning hotter and hotter, until they melted together.

Lava.

Fused.

Flowing into each other.

Becoming one.

As the world erupted around them.

After, they rested in the deliciously sharp contrasts of making love—fury and delicacy, tenderness and force, hunger and satiation—all living in complete harmony within the same exquisite moments.

Meg touched Morgan's face with the pure wonder of one who had thought they would never be whole again, a half-living person who had been restored to life.

She contemplated the fact that they had made love in some of the most luxurious places in the world. They had made love on silk sheets with rose petals being crushed around them.

But nothing matched the intensity of the experience they had just shared. In an open-air shelter with rain sluicing off the roof, on a picnic table with chickens roosting under it. It had felt bold and yet also vulnerable. And Meg thought that perhaps it was the very vulnerability—physical, emotional, spiritual—that had made the love-making so exquisite.

Gently, gently, gently, Morgan gathered her.

He lifted her nakedness to his own, cradled her against him, walked out into the rain, and held her up to it, as if she was a virgin being sacrificed on the altar of desire.

The warm rain on her skin, his touch, sang across her heightened awareness, a bow to taut strings, turning her to music.

Finally, he set her down and they raced, hand in hand, down the bank into the pool. Just this morning, a trickle had gurgled over those rocks, but now it was a torrent.

Nonetheless, they stood beneath it, letting the natural forces that had brought them together scrub them clean.

At first, the heat of their experience kept them warm, but then that dwindled, and Meg felt suddenly cold. She shivered, and Morgan took her hand and led her back to the picnic shelter.

Quickly, he began opening the clothing packages.

"Hey," she protested, through chattering teeth, "those are for the wedding."

He took one of the white T-shirts and came and stood before her. He began, methodically, tenderly to dry her.

"White T-shirts are a dime a dozen," he assured her. "We'll replace them."

And so she surrendered to his ministrations, to his wringing water from her hair, and tousling it dry, journeying downward over her body. Morgan's touch was efficient, and yet there was an element of reverence to it, as if she was an altar he worshiped at.

And when he was done, she took the T-shirt from him, and dried him off, glorying in the look and feel of his flawless skin, his beautiful body, the wonderful familiarity of it all.

When she was finished, Morgan turned again to the open packages, dropped a dry T-shirt over her head. It came to her thigh, like a minidress. He pulled on a pair of the black shorts.

And then they lay down on top of the picnic table, side by side, she nestled under the shelter of his arm. Considering how hard that surface was, it felt to her like a feather bed. Because he was there. Because she could feel the beat of his heart, and the heat of his skin, and in this moment, everything felt so incredibly right in her world.

They listened to the steady drum of the rain on the shelter roof, and his breathing was so steady and strong. She thought he might have gone to sleep.

But, he hadn't.

"I wonder what you're going to tell Marjorie," she said.

He let out a huff of annoyance. "There is no Marjorie. Really, Meg? You don't know me any better than that? You think I'd cheat on some-one?"

"I'm sorry. She wasn't right for you, anyway."

"How would you know?"

"She didn't like children."

"How would you know she didn't like chil-dren?"

"Because I asked you, and you didn't know. You always know if people like children."

"This may strike you as odd, but we hardly went to the playground on our dates."

"You don't have to go to a playground," she said. "It's in the way they cock their head when they hear a child's laughter, or the little smile on their face when they see a child on a bicycle with training wheels."

The way they look when a little boy shows them his pet chicken.

His fingers came to life, played sweetly with a tangle in her damp hair.

"Why wouldn't you even talk to me, Meg?" he finally asked gruffly, and yet she heard the pain in his voice, and felt the sting of how she had be-haved. She knew it could be perceived as cruel.

There was no point in telling him she had suf-fered, too. None.

Talk to him? How could she? The sound of his voice would have weakened her resolve at a time when she most needed to be strong.

For him.

There was an expression—maybe part of a song—*cruel to be kind*.

"I couldn't," she said, and that was the truth.

His chest heaved under where her cheek was laid against it.

"There's things we need to talk about," he said. "Logistical things."

If her refuge was art, this was his. Logistics. The science of making things work.

"Such as?"

"Have you looked at the separation agreement?"

He took her silence as an answer. He sighed. "Have you even got a lawyer?"

A lawyer? To deal with Morgan? It made sense, of course. It would be a good way to keep her distance while the *logistics* were looked after. And yet, the very thought of using a lawyer to communicate with Morgan turned her stomach.

She considered the possibility that legal representation, advice, paper, documents, made everything permanent and irrevocable.

But isn't that what needed to happen? Exactly?

Was she not taking the next steps because she hoped she would weaken? That this would all be a nightmare that she could put behind her?

Wasn't this, after all, enough? To be together? To live in the ecstasy that came from being in one another's arms?

No! Nature had assigned a purpose to what had just transpired between them! The purpose was the children she could not give him. That he needed, desperately, to make his life what it had once been.

Whole. Happy.

"You're entitled to half," he said. His fingers had stopped playing in her hair.

"I don't want half, Morgan."

"Oh, right," he said, and the faintest bitterness closed in around the edges of the beautiful afterglow. "You can't handle the lifestyle. Still, in our province, there's a legal requirement. You get half. I don't care what you do with it. Give it to a charity if you can't handle it."

That's what she would do, she decided. She would give it to a charity. His charity.

"How is everything at Out of the Ashes?" she asked him.

Her question made Morgan contemplate the twists and turns of life. Once, his life had seemed entirely predictable.

And then the fire had come, torn through the beloved family cottage and taken his brother, his sister-in-law and his niece and nephew, a harsh reminder that chaos waited at the gates of the most ordered of lives. A man thinking life was predictable was the grandest of illusions.

He'd met Meg at her first art show, in an up-scale gallery in Vancouver. He'd stood before her painting *Out of the Ashes*, and he had felt the most dangerous thing of all.

Hope.

The painting depicted a burned-out hull of a building with one tender sapling growing out of the rubble. Against that grim backdrop, the new tree was reaching its tender, brilliant green leaves toward a bright sun.

He had been shocked at the coincidence that the painting bore the same name as the charity he had just started to honor his lost family members.

He had purchased the painting with a sense of urgency, needing to have it before someone else snapped it up. He knew that this work of art would become the official image of his fledgling charity.

"Would you like to meet the artist?" the gallery owner had asked him.

And then she was there. Shy. Blond hair swept up around an exquisite, delicate face. Green eyes huge, promising incredible depth of spirit. She'd been wearing a simple black dress, no jewelry and hardly any makeup. She kept tugging at the hem of that dress, self-consciously, as if she didn't have the most beautiful legs in the room.

Possibly in all of Vancouver.

Meg Lawson had been extraordinarily beautiful, and totally unaware of her beauty. From the moment his eyes had connected with hers, he had felt it. Her incredible intensity.

The earth moving under his feet.

That sapling within him, pushing relentlessly through the rubble that was his heart. He had allowed himself—foolishly, it seemed now—to hope.

He had allowed himself to believe he and Meg could rebuild. Not replace what he had lost but honor it.

As it turned out, she had losses, too.

The loss of her brother, just like him.

They understood each other in ways that no other person could. She alleviated the deep loneliness his walk with sorrow had caused him.

They had slowly uncovered each other's stories. Hers was filled with tragedy. The brother with a disability, the single mom, spirit-numbing poverty and challenges, the death of the brother, and her mom's slide into despair and addiction.

He understood that kind of despair that her mother suffered, and at the same time, Meg allowed him to see how much he had to be grateful for.

He had known the security of love and family, he had been so sure in his knowledge of it that he had taken it for granted.

When he shared stories of his family with her, he saw her deep longing for what he had always had.

And he thought he could give it to her. They longed, after all, for exactly the same thing, though they came at that longing from different directions.

He wanted what he once had with a desperation that frightened him.

She longed for what she had never had with equal desperation.

They both wanted a family.

That place to call home, the destination the heart longed for, where you were secure in your place, where you felt safe, protected, accepted, valued.

But then Meg, the one he was counting on to be his partner as he reengaged in the journey of life, had just become another bitter reminder of how unpredictable that life was, and what a terrible force hope could be, like a fickle woman, teasing, promising, then withdrawing.

He'd just made love to his wife in the fury of a storm. A case in point about life's unpredictability. Because he could not have predicted this moment, and if he had been able to, he would have predicted that he had the strength to resist it.

"How is everything at Out of the Ashes?" she asked, again.

"We're going to build a children's camp on part of the land around Sarah's Reach," he told her. "That's what should be there. When I think of the sound of children's laughter over that lake again, it makes me feel—"

How much was he willing to reveal to her? It made him feel less wounded. It made him feel as if good could come from bad. It made him feel as if he wasn't completely powerless in the face of tragedy. That he could do something.

"Good." He finished his sentence abruptly.

Her hand squeezed his. He wanted to jerk it away, at the same time he wanted this moment with her.

Maybe even needed it.

A beggar satisfied with any kind of crumb.

"What's going on with your art?" he asked her, sliding his hand from hers.

If only it was so easy to pull his heart away.

Meg felt him pull his hand away.

She contemplated what Morgan had just told her. It emphasized, really, how important and how correct her decision had been.

She knew when he had hesitated over finishing that line about how he felt. He had almost said *happy*.

And then he had deliberately watered it down.

Still, she knew the truth. When Morgan thought

of happiness, whether he was aware of it or not, he thought of children.

What she could not give him.

And the subject that haunted her paintings, now. The gallery she was working with in Ottawa was begging for new things.

But she could not part with her most recent work. Not yet.

They were of families, mostly beach scenes. Children, focused intently on buckets and shovels, a baby under an umbrella with mom and dad, she reading a book while he kept an eye on the kids.

Her favorite was one of two young boys on a wooden platform-style float, out in a lake, pushing each other into the water, one captured forever, head thrown back in laughter, arms flailing, midair, about to hit the water.

Meg was aware she had never experienced anything like that.

Morgan's longing was her longing, too. She was painting not what she knew, but what she had hoped for.

What he knew.

And what he would have again if she could just be strong enough.

Without warning, a chicken, with a great flapping of wings, got itself up on the table with them.

It settled in the middle of Morgan's naked belly.

It broke, thankfully, whatever intensity had been building between them, and he sat up, laughing. Meg sat up beside him.

The chicken slid away, but sat beside him, and then cocked its head, regarded him, and jumped right onto his lap, settling itself again.

His hands closed around it, stroking it.

Meg looked at his face, and the small smile that played across the curve of the lips that had just possessed her.

In his unguarded expression, she could see every single thing the chicken, by instinct, sensed.

Such a good man. Strong, gentle, caring.

Her heart felt as if it would break when she thought of how he would have looked holding their baby.

Could she paint that? A father looking down at the miracle of the child he had helped create, the child he had made a decision to bring into the world?

She didn't think she could paint that. And on the other hand, is that not what painting was about?

Capturing the essential moments of life?

Watching him with that chicken just confirmed what she already knew. There were things that were essential to Morgan's life that she could not give him.

And then, as abruptly as it had begun, the rain stopped.

The sun came out, and rainbows danced at the edges of that waterfall they had stood naked beneath. Birds called out, and the chicken in Morgan's lap stretched out its wings, clucked fondly, and then leaped from his lap. The water dripped—*plop, plop, plop*—off the edges of the roof, and the soaked leathery leaves of the jungle-like foliage around them.

And then, Morgan cocked his head. "Someone's coming."

She sensed a change in his whole demeanor, his armor sliding back into place. At first she didn't hear anything, but then she heard voices coming from the direction of the resort.

He reached into the open packet of clothes, and handed her a pair of shorts, and he pulled on one of the white T-shirts.

They were dressed just in the nick of time, too.

A small army of golf carts, led by Keona, came around a twist in the trail. Jonathon was driving another one, all the groomsmen riding with him.

They stopped at the first washout, and the men, armed with shovels, all hopped out of the golf carts and cleared the mud and debris within seconds.

This was one of the most admirable things about Jonathon and Morgan and the group of guys they hung out with. Despite being amongst the wealthiest people in the world, they all carried an air of humility about them. They were hardworking, willing to do what it took to get the job done.

As the rescue team got back on their golf carts, Morgan turned to her.

"I'm sorry," he said, his voice a low growl. "That was a new low. Taking advantage of a woman after she's had a couple drinks."

Meg felt as if he had slapped her. What had happened between them was a new low? What had happened between them needed an apology?

"I was not—am not—drunk," she snapped, but the little army of golf carts arrived before she could pursue it further.

Jonathon and the others came toward them. Jon was a good-looking man, tall and well-built, his coloring dark like Caylee's.

They were going to make beautiful, curly-haired babies with enormous brown eyes.

Babies.

Again she thought of that. The gift she could not ever give Morgan. It should have given her an imperative reason to resist all her impulses.

Morgan had been right. She may not have been drunk, but certainly her inhibitions had fled her. Participating in that dance hadn't helped. It had put her in touch with her sensual side, unleashed her desires, made her eager to embrace everything it meant to be a woman.

As if just being with him wasn't enough to do that.

Jonathon took them in with a quick glance.

"Matching outfits," he said with a raise of his eyebrow. "Cute. Like the von Trapp family singers wearing their matching curtains."

"We were soaked. We changed." Morgan's tone did not invite more questioning.

Meg was sure what had just transpired between her and Morgan was written all over their faces—like guilty children with the chocolate from the stolen cookies smeared around their lips—but all she saw in Jonathon's face, underlying his teasing tone, was relief that they were safe.

And if he suspected something had transpired between them, their friend was likely nothing but happy about it.

"Beginning to think the wedding is cursed," Jonathon said good-naturedly, clapping Morgan on the shoulder and wrapping her in a quick, hard hug.

"It's me," she said. "I'm cursed. Whenever I

travel to a new place you can count on bad things happening."

Jonathon gave her a bemused look. "Really? All the events of the world fall on your shoulders?"

When he put it like that, it did seem ridiculous.

"Flash flood warnings started coming on our phones and we realized you two were unaccounted for."

The guys quickly enveloped them, joking about them being pranked for a survival show. Apparently, they had hoped to find Morgan in a loin cloth, and Meg roasting a freshly caught chicken over a spit.

She *loved* the camaraderie Morgan had with his friends. It was one of the ways she had managed to stop herself from going back to him.

Knowing he was surrounded with *this*.

Back-clapping, and boisterous laughter, and teasing, and underneath all that, running so deep, the strength of men's friendships.

"Have Caylee's parents arrived?" Meg asked Jonathon when the noise had settled down a bit.

"No parents, no wedding regalia."

"At least we have a backup plan for that," Meg said.

"Caylee showed me the pictures. You missed your calling, Meggie, you could be one of those bloggers or influencers or whatever they're called this week."

He put his hands on his hips, leaned toward her and did the pursing thing with his lips.

She laughed, but she noticed Morgan didn't.

"Mr. and Mrs. Hart," Keona said, pulling up to them.

Jonathon raised an eyebrow when neither of them corrected him, but Morgan deflected. "Please. Just Morgan."

"And Meg," she agreed quickly.

Was she blushing? Was what had transpired between them obvious to a casual observer? Would Morgan think it was amusing, like two high school kids caught necking behind the athletics storage shed?

She glanced at his face and swallowed.

He had not laughed at Jonathon's lighthearted imitation of her, and did not seem to think this was funny, at all.

In fact, as the passion that had caught like fire between them was doused, Morgan's expression was distinctly grim.

"Thank goodness you're all right," Keona said. "We've been trying to text you."

The last thing either of them had been doing was checking their phones over the last hour or so!

"Is everyone else accounted for?" Morgan

asked, always *that* guy, who understood priorities, who was genuinely concerned about others.

"We have one other couple trapped on the other side of that," Keona nodded toward where mud clogged the road behind them. "But they've been texting us."

"You guys can head back," Jonathon said. "I'll help dig out."

They said nothing as they gathered their packages and then followed Keona to where a large group of men were muscling their golf cart off the rock it had lodged on. Once successful, one of them took it for a quick spin to make sure it was still in working order.

Meg hated it that Morgan wouldn't look at her.

As if they were Adam and Eve in the garden, and they had just tasted the forbidden fruit.

And he was ashamed of the weakness that had driven him to it.

"Can you drive the cart back yourself?" Morgan asked her. "I'd like to help dig out, too."

"Of course," she said. But she read in between the lines.

He probably did want to help out. He and Jonathon would always be those two guys you could rely on to be decent. But Meg suspected Morgan's desire to help out was not nearly as strong as his desire to get away from her.

Well, she'd show him she wanted to get away from him, too!

She stepped on the accelerator of the golf cart. Rather than making a graceful exit, it jerked unbecomingly for several feet, stalled, jerked again, and then, rather than sweeping away, she trundled off to the snickers of the road crew behind her.

Meg drove herself back to the resort, marveling at how the sun was shining again. Except for the occasional palm frond lying across the path, Kauai was once more a tropical paradise, as if nothing had happened.

Meg was well aware it wasn't going to be as easy for her and Morgan to pretend their private storm had not happened.

She parked the golf cart and gathered the packages.

Caylee practically fell on her as she made her way down the path.

"I've been so worried."

Her friend held her back and looked at her appraisingly. "Have you been drinking?"

Oh, geez. "A bit. By accident. I didn't know it had so much alcohol in it."

Caylee cocked her head. "I'm not sure that's what's causing that look."

"What look?"

"You look—" Caylee paused, searching for the right word.

"What?" she snapped.

"Radiant!"

"Snatching your life back from the jaws of death will do that for you."

"Was it terrifying?"

She thought of Morgan's lips on her, of the passion between them, of how she was going to keep that at bay for another few days.

"Terrifying," she agreed.

"When that rain started to come down, the first thing I wondered was where you and Morgan were. The box with the wedding clothes in it was found. It nearly got here, but then the plane had to divert because of the storm. Our wedding clothes are sitting on the Big Island at the moment."

"Oh, dear."

"And Mom and Dad are getting closer! San Francisco, at the moment. The storm here is what has delayed them now."

"They have to get here!"

Caylee flapped a hand languidly, again astonishing Meg with her laid-back attitude. "What will be will be. That's *aloha* apparently. Go have a shower and then come to my cottage and let me look at what you got. And then let's hook up with the rest of my entourage—"

They both giggled at the fact a girl from their neighborhood had an entourage!

"—and then go to the spa. We're glamming up for the wedding. The whole deal—manicures, pedicures and facials!"

And then they giggled again, because they both came from a neighborhood where people not only did not have entourages, but they didn't even work at the spa. They worked at big-box stores, and in housekeeping at care homes. The spa? They sneered at those high-and-mighty snobby, pampered types, while maybe harboring a secret envy.

Caylee looped her arm through Meg's and it felt, impossibly and deliciously, as if everything was okay in the world.

CHAPTER ELEVEN

AN HOUR OR so later, the five women of the wedding party—the entourage, as Caylee was now calling them—had all gathered in Caylee's cottage. One thing that Meg had never expected when she had packed her bag and moved across the country was how much she would miss her friends.

Most of these women had been her circle—just as Morgan had his circle—since she had still been in her teens.

Meg and Caylee had known each other since first grade. They had met Samantha at a throw-together beach volleyball game when they were all just out of high school. The boys they had been trying to impress that day were but a memory, but the friendship had stood the test of time.

A year or so later, Allie had joined them after a hysterical night at a karaoke bar. Her rendition of "My Heart Is a Stone" could set cats within a one-mile radius into a caterwauling competition with her. After three glasses of wine, it still didn't take any coaxing at all to get her to sing it.

Becky, the quietest of them, was a writer whom Meg had met through artsy circles. The five of them had an unbreakable bond. They had each other's backs through it all, and there had been so much that had happened to them all in the seven or so years they had hung out together.

A lot of it involved men, of course: hookups, breakups, makeups.

But a lot of it didn't. Becky had her first children's book published. Meg had done the illustrations for it. What a celebration that had been! And for at least a year after, every member of that group was selling copies to strangers on the subway out of their purses.

Samantha graduated from university and was working for the best law firm in the city.

Allie had started the most amazing cosmetics company. It had flopped spectacularly, but still, it had been amazing! She was doing something with interior design now.

Caylee got her dream job with an event planning company, and had been able to put all her skills to use on her own wedding.

For a long time, Meg had worked as a cashier at a grocery store. Besides having illustrated Becky's book, she didn't do very well with her dream, which was pursuing a career in art.

But then, she sold a few pieces. And then a few more. When a gallery took some of her things on commission, this group of women had made sure that gallery was swarmed.

A year later, she'd had her own show.

And been introduced to Morgan Hart, who wanted one of her paintings to become the official symbol for his charity Out of the Ashes.

Meg shook off that memory, and replaced it with precious ones with girlfriends. Caylee had instigated Adventure Club and they'd taken turns coming up with ideas. Rock climbing, white water rafting, a cattle drive, skydiving.

And yet it was the most simple moments of friendship that shone: admiring somebody's new kitten or kitchen set, watching movies, conducting a book club, grabbing lunch downtown, spending nights at home with a few bottles of wine and guaranteed laughter.

And those friends had meant there was always someone to catch the tears.

Allie had had an accidental pregnancy, as a result of a one-night stand. The guy had been a jerk about it, and all of them had sworn they would be that baby's family. They had talked and dreamed and bought adorable clothes and planned a nursery. And all of them had been equally heartbroken when she miscarried.

Becky had lost her mother after a long battle with cancer.

Samantha had found out her fiancé of four years was a serial cheater.

They had all been a bit shocked that it was Meg who had been the first to get married. And oh, the catch that Morgan Hart was! They had *all* loved him. After the awful experiences Samantha and Allie had had, it had restored some hope to them.

Love was out there!

Then Jonathon had taken up with Caylee and they—independent, career-oriented, adventurous women that they were—had been in absolute delirious fits of joy that happily-ever-after really happened to ordinary women like them.

Meg had not been aware how much she needed these women, her friends, until she had made the choice to leave the warmth of that circle behind her when she left her marriage.

Really, when she needed them most, she had chosen to go alone.

She had chosen a terrible, lonely route for herself.

And her friends had been hurt and angry—not because she had destroyed their newly nurtured hopes in fairy tales—but because they had needed to be there for her.

But how, with all that love around her, could

she have kept the secret of *why*? How long before, in a moment of weakness, she confided in one of them?

She trusted them completely. Almost.

Each one, in their own way, would think they knew what was best for her. Which one of them would have felt compelled to share her secret with Morgan?

Maybe none of them would have.

But it was a chance Meg had not been prepared to take.

Instead, she had deliberately moved away from the temptation of being loved by them. She had nursed her broken heart alone. No one to knock on her door and say—steaming hot lasagna from Pargarios in hand—"Have you eaten?"

No one to bring over a bottle of wine. Or two. Or three.

No one to say "How about bull riding for our next adventure? Or an electric-bike tour of Napa?"

No one to suggest a marathon of sad movies to let the dam of tears burst. Was there anything better, in the whole world, than five women bawling their eyes out at the end of *The Other Side of the Mountain*?

Well, maybe one thing better.

And Meg had just done that one thing with Morgan.

She wondered if these sisters of her heart knew. Or suspected. She felt as if the passionate encounter she had just had with her ex was written all over her.

But they, thankfully, were preoccupied with all things wedding. The topic of Morgan and her failed marriage—and the awkwardness of Meg's reunion with Morgan—were carefully avoided. This led Meg to suspect they might have discussed their strategy in dealing with her beforehand.

Today, only fun, lighthearted wedding stuff was allowed. Caylee tried on the backup bridal dress, and the rest of them all tried on their wine-colored sundresses. They took turns at the mirror and took pictures of each other and oohed and aahed. The focus, interestingly, was not really on the bride nor on the replacement dresses. Instead, each of her friends made it all about Meg and her great taste and her artist's eye, and now much they all missed her.

Their love and acceptance was like water to a person who had crawled across the desert, sunlight to a person who had been locked away in darkness.

By the time they all linked arms and headed to the spa, Meg told herself she had put the romantic afternoon interlude with Morgan behind her.

"Meg has highly recommended a drink called

Pining for You," Caylee told the person taking their drink orders. "One for everybody."

As they lay there on white-sheeted beds, open to the ocean, avocado masks on their faces, Meg was so aware of one thing.

She and Morgan would be together again tonight. Unless, finally, flights were leaving Kauai? Shouldn't she really be checking the availability of a different room instead of lying here, relishing her state of absolute decadence and wallowing in the love of friends she had missed so much?

Aloha, Caylee had said with a wave of her hand. *What will be will be.*

Meg had never been much of a *what will be will be* kind of a person. She liked control. On the other hand, Caylee had never been that person, either, and look at her now after just a few days here.

Kamelei had suggested if you stayed here long enough, you could understand the concept.

So for now, Meg was just going to give herself over to enjoying the experience, even as she acknowledged at least part of her enjoyment was not because of being surrounded by the love of her friends.

It was because Morgan had coaxed a part of her back to life.

The most dangerous part.

The spark was glowing.

Waiting. An ember that could flicker, then sputter, then gain strength and then roar. A little tiny spark, and a whisper of a breath on it, was all it took to burn a whole world down.

So easy to dismiss that with the turquoise water in the distance, the sounds of waves and chickens and birds, lulling her.

Into a sense that everything could be okay.

She did not touch the slushy drink beside her.

Because if things did unfold, again, between them, she was not going to give Morgan the opportunity to blame it on a Sugarloaf White pineapple slushy.

Though, ironically, the blame could be laid squarely at the feet of one thing.

For eight long months she had been pining for Morgan.

Ridiculous to believe everything would be okay, for even one second, in the face of all the evidence of how wrong things could go. Look how her world had collapsed beyond repair the day that doctor had given her the news.

And yet, lying there on that massage bed, naively, stupidly, happily, believe it she did.

She was not unaware that the fact she had made love with her husband had a great deal to do with this rosy feeling of well-being.

She could let the fact that this was only the briefest respite in her dark journey overshadow that.

Or she could surrender to *aloha*.

And just let whatever happened, happen.

And Meg hoped that involved Morgan's arms wrapping around her—and quite a bit more—again.

Morgan came back to the resort with his friends. They were all tired and dirty, and somehow it felt as if clearing that pathway of storm debris had turned into the best prelude to a bachelor party ever.

It also meant he did not have to encounter Meg. Tonight, Caylee had scheduled the guys and girls in separate camps. Girls were at the spa, prepping fingers and toes and faces for the big day. Then they were planning dinner together and having a kind of bachelorette party.

So the guys ended up roughhousing by the pool. A couple of them had too much to drink, and the party moved to Ralph's bungalow. They ordered pizza from the resort's wood-fired oven, and found a football game to watch on pay-per-view TV.

Which Morgan was fine with, because once he went back to that bungalow, how the hell was he going to act normal around Meg?

He wasn't entirely sure what happened at a bachelorette party, and he hoped it didn't involve male dancers. Because if Meg was building on those pineapple slushies of earlier, that could lead to trouble. She had no idea how beautiful she was, but guys got it. Look at that drink that had been sent her way by a complete stranger.

She wasn't, Morgan told himself firmly, *that kind of girl.*

Of course, her abandonment had left him with the distressing knowledge he didn't know her nearly as well as he thought he did. And that dance she had done seemed as if it had revealed all her secrets.

How she behaved with male dancers was none of his business, Morgan told himself sternly. The fact that just thinking about it made him feel faintly angry and faintly protective meant he was already in big trouble.

Hadn't he proven this afternoon that what she most needed protecting from was probably him? One thing he knew for sure, *that* was not happening again.

His phone rang partway through the game. Caylee. He answered way too fast.

"Thank you for shopping today. Spectacular choices."

"I hope we don't need the backup plan," he

said. "Any sign of the real deal?" He listened for sounds of music. Rowdiness. *Male dancers.*

"On the Big Island. Supposed to be here tomorrow."

"That's cutting it close. Your parents?" He heard women laughing.

"San Francisco at the moment. Fingers crossed they'll be here tomorrow night."

"You must be a nervous wreck."

"Oddly enough, not. Maybe because Meg has introduced us all to the most amazing concoction." She giggled. "Pineappling for You."

That was all he needed to know!

CHAPTER TWELVE

IF THE LADIES were imbibing the pineapple slush-ies, Morgan knew he had to stay away from Huipu—and Meg—tonight.

Despite telling himself it was none of his business, he heard himself asking what they were planning next for the evening ahead.

"Oh, I'm dragging the ladies away from the slushies now. Nobody's allowed to stumble around and wreck their newly polished toes! Besides, everyone's tired, and you said your plan for tomorrow starts early."

"Sunrise," Morgan reminded her. "Meet on the beach. Don't eat first."

"Sunrise breakfast on the beach!" Caylee said, delighted. "Morgan, you're just the best guy."

"Well, that's why I'm called the best man," he said dryly.

He could hear giggling behind Caylee.

She lowered her voice. "I meant you're the best guy as in *how could anyone let you get away*?"

Meg hadn't let him get away. She'd thrown him back.

But there was absolutely no point arguing semantics with anyone who had indulged in an unknown number of Sugarloaf White pineapple libations.

"Bring a bathing suit," he said, ignoring her invitation to commiserate with her over the unfairness of his wife abandoning him when he was clearly perfect.

"Ladies," Caylee called, "the dress of the day for tomorrow is bikinis. Morgan says the teenier the better."

"I did not say that!" he called, hopefully loud enough for all of them to hear him. Sheesh.

"Ha ha," one of women yelled out. He thought he recognized Becky's voice. She was generally shy which, unfortunately, underscored the inhibition-releasing powers of Pining for You.

"I bet Meg doesn't even own a bikini." This caused raucous laughter and more rowdiness.

"It's just the women there, right?" Morgan asked, against his own orders to himself not to.

"Who else would be here?" Caylee responded, startled.

"I don't know. Sometimes you hear of things getting a little wild and crazy at the bachelorette party."

Silence. "In what way?"

Stop, he ordered himself. "Like in the Mad Mike way."

"Mad Mike?"

He should leave it. He still had a chance to save his dignity. On the other hand, what if Meg needed saving?

"Those guys," he said tersely, "that take their shirts off. And more. While dancing."

"I think you mean Magic," she said dryly. "Are you asking if I have male strippers lined up for my bachelorette party?"

She said that way too loud, and behind her he could hear squeals of what could only be interpreted as excitement.

"Sorry, ladies," she called, "I'm afraid the craziest thing here was avocado masks."

He didn't want to admit, even to himself, how relieved he was.

"Let's stream *that* movie next!" Was that Becky again? Who knew about her secret side?

On that note, Morgan disconnected and put away his phone.

His relief was short lived. What was he going to do about tonight? He'd had enough danger for one day. He was not going back to Huipu to deal with Meg pining for him. But only when her guard was down. Or maybe watched a sexy movie.

The rest of the time, it was *so long, Morgan, have a nice life.*

He ended up sleeping on Ralph's couch. Not because he was drunk, though if people wanted to think that, they could.

He lay awake staring at the ceiling, thinking of her soaked hair, and the feel of her skin and the way her eyes had looked.

She loved him.

But he'd always known that. It only deepened the torment to wonder why—when it was so evident how she felt—she had left him?

It seemed to Morgan he had just gone to sleep when those damn chickens started crowing. He got up feeling not as if there was a great day ahead for him to anticipate, but as if he was a warrior strapping on his armor for battle.

And somehow he wasn't ready for the first battle being going over there to find something to wear, to face Meg in the intimacy of that cottage, sharing the bathroom, going into a shower that still smelled of her.

He stepped over Keith, who was on the floor, and went down to the beach in the predawn darkness. He'd heard the ocean was full of sharks at this time of day. He could only hope!

Fighting off sharks seemed preferable—not to mention easier—than fighting off his attraction to the wife who'd abandoned him.

He stripped off his rumpled shirt and dived into the waves. Swimming in the salty water, with the stars evaporating from the sky above him, Morgan felt as if his strength was restored to him. He felt his resolve hardening.

He wasn't going to beg Meg for an answer as to how she could love him and leave him. What if she denied loving him? Wasn't he in enough pain already?

He wasn't going to fall under her spell again, either. Nothing good lay that way. He had only one mission. He was the best man. It was his job to make sure this wedding went off without a hitch, which included tension, in any variety, particularly between he and Meg.

He only had to get through today. His surprise. And then tomorrow, the wedding. Caylee and Jonathon would be off to the most secluded seaside bungalow Hale Iwa Kai had. But they had invited their guests to enjoy the resort for three more days after the wedding.

Still, nothing said Morgan had to stay. His best man duties would be officially ended. He could make his excuses and leave.

So, two more days of Meg.

Anybody could swear off anything for two days. In the span of the cosmos that was nothing. A speck of dust.

After his swim, he sat on the beach, his arms folded around his knees, and watched as the world around him came to light. It was beautiful and for a moment his troubles and torments seemed as miniscule as that cosmic speck of dust that was time.

One by one, the other members of the group joined him. He was so aware when Meg came, in an oversize sun hat, dark glasses and a swim cover-up.

If anybody thought it was unusual that he was wet and shirtless, they didn't comment. He suspected, like him, they were caught in the complete enchantment of a new day beginning in this mystical land.

Only Meg would know the shirt lying beside him in the sand was the same one he had worn yesterday, familiar with it because she had peeled it from him. Meg noticed details, regardless. It was part of her artistic nature.

In fact, when he slid her a glance, Meg did seem to be taking in the details of his naked chest with way too much interest! He picked up the shirt—crumpled as it was—and put it on. He should have shaken it first. It was full of sand. She raised an eyebrow at him.

"Where's the promised feast?" Jonathon growled. "We're starving."

"I don't see anything to eat," Caylee said, looking up and down the empty beach, her hands on her hips. "We've been summoned here under false pretenses. Let's throw Morgan into the ocean."

"He's already been in. It's not as if we're throwing him off an ice floe in Antarctica," Ralph pointed out.

But why let the facts spoil a good dunking? It was too late. His buddies grabbed him, two on his arms and two on his legs and splashed out into the surf with him to give him the old heave-ho. Everybody was laughing. He found himself laughing, too.

How long since he had laughed?

Allowed himself to feel like a part of something?

It felt more than good. It felt wonderful.

And despite all his guards, and all his best efforts, did he link this ability to laugh, to feel wonderful, to yesterday and to the part of him Meg had unleashed?

The part of him that wanted to live?

"What is that?" Becky asked before the count to three was completed.

The guys released him without tossing him to the sea, and everyone turned toward a sailboat coming into the cove.

"That," Morgan said, "is breakfast. In fact, we're going to spend the whole day on the Melo-Melo."

His surprise for the wedding party was a private charter of a sixty-five-foot powered catamaran that also worked under sail, if the winds were right. Booking the super luxury yacht had, admittedly, been a bit of a dig at Meg. *You think can't handle the lifestyle?*

Check this out.

Okay, maybe he even hoped to make her sorry for everything she had left behind.

Though his motives weren't all tainted by Meg.

"Apparently the only way to experience the true majesty of the Napali Coast is from the ocean," he explained to the group. "The Melo-Melo will give us the best vantage point, plus there's planned stops at famous snorkeling spots, including Lehua Crater, and one off the Forbidden Island of Niihau."

"Why's it called forbidden?" Caylee asked.

Good question. Did forbidden things happen there? His mind drifted to the forbidden thing he'd indulged in yesterday. He deferred to his phone. Meg was watching him closely, as if she knew where his mind had gone.

"'It was closed to visitors during a polio epidemic to safeguard the residents, and that's when it became known as the Forbidden Island,'" he read, "'but even before that the family that bought it from King Kamehameha in the 1800s promised to preserve Hawaiian culture and language, so development and visitors have always been limited.'"

"Oh," Caylee cried, as the vessel launched

boats to come and get them. "Morgan! It couldn't be more perfect. What a wonderful foil to all the frazzle of the last few days."

See? It was that easy to be the best man. He had made the bride happy and that was all that counted. Wasn't it?

CHAPTER THIRTEEN

MEG HAD TROUBLE keeping her eyes off her shirt-less ex-husband. That interlude yesterday had made her feel as if she was starving—and not for breakfast, either.

She had lain awake waiting for him to come back to their suite. She had deliberately refused drinks at the spa. She was determined Morgan wasn't going to regret their lovemaking this time. He wasn't going to blame it on her being under the influence.

She knew she was playing with fire.

But she couldn't stop herself. What if she never saw him again after this wedding? What if they signed those papers and went their separate ways?

Oh, sure, they'd probably meet at weddings. And anniversaries. Birthday parties.

Showers, baptisms, those events that celebrated what she couldn't give him.

But life might never hand them this again: this opportunity to be so intensely together. She knew it was wrong to want him so badly. She knew it was wrong to give in to the temptation to touch him, to taste him, to possess him.

To have him possess her.

But she was like an addict who had been promised one more spectacular fix before heading into a life of abstinence.

She was an addict who wanted one more chance not to feel pain.

She wanted just one more memory to carry into a bleak, lonely, future with her.

But looking at Morgan, in the same shorts he had worn yesterday, his rumpled shirt, also from yesterday, she recognized they were at cross-purposes. He had obviously slept on someone's couch to avoid her.

And of course, he was right.

Of course that was the reasonable thing to do.

And yet, watching that sailboat pull into the cove, the wind filling the vibrant colors of its billowing sails, Meg surrendered to the sensation of being in a place of pure magic.

Where anything could—and would—happen. *Had* happened.

Consequences be damned. Consequences belonged in that world she would go back to. And she would be there for a very long time.

Here? Here she had—she counted them on her fingers—five more days. Today, the wed-

ding tomorrow, and three days following that.
She felt like someone who had been given a life
sentence ordering their last meal, being given
one more chance to experience the fullness and
the vibrancy of life itself.

She was suddenly glad that, underneath her
very modest swim cover, was the bathing suit
Caylee had talked her into borrowing.

Becky had been quite right last night. Meg
did not own a bikini. She owned practical one-
piece bathing suits with racing backs that were
made for swimming.

Caylee had opened her closet to an assort-
ment of bathing suits, most purchased just for
her Hawaiian honeymoon. None of them had
been worn, and in fact, most of them still had
the price tags on them.

Her circle of friends had insisted Meg try on
half a dozen of the skimpiest numbers.

The try-ons had stopped when she had put on
the one she now had on underneath her swim
cover.

It was black. It was tiny. It was the kind of
swimsuit that was featured in that famous Feb-
ruary issue of the sports magazine.

When she had looked at herself in it, she had
expected to feel utterly ridiculous. Instead, Meg
had felt, fully, her own power.

She had known Morgan didn't have a chance.

And yet, standing here on the beach, watching boats come in to pick them up and ferry them out to the MeloMelo, she felt a sudden flagging—not her mission, but her courage to accomplish it.

The dilemma: she couldn't have him if she'd been drinking. He'd made that clear.

And yet she wasn't sure how she'd find the nerve to get out of the swimsuit cover without a little liquid encouragement.

In fact, she needn't have worried. She was soon totally immersed in exactly the lifestyle she had told Morgan she couldn't handle.

What was to handle? Meg mused. There were more staff members than guests on the incredible yacht, catering to their every whim. The excursion Morgan was treating the wedding party to seemed to be designed around one goal and one goal only, and that was to give the clients an experience of pure bliss.

Breakfast on the deck of the MeloMelo consisted of an amazing selection of rare cheeses, local fruits, freshly baked croissants and just-squeezed orange juice, with or without a splash of champagne.

The delectable feast was served on fine china with real silverware. As they enjoyed breakfast, they passed the longest stretch of beach in Hawaii, Polihale. Then they began to see the wonders of the Napali coastline, which cruise leader Leilani referred to as *sacred*.

Indeed, Meg had a deep sense of the sacred all around her as she listened to Leilani explain how this geographical marvel had been created by five million years of volcanic activity and erosion.

Five million years. It gave Meg a sense of her own struggles—and even her own existence—being put in perspective.

They cruised by four-thousand-foot cliffs, hidden beaches, deep sea caves and breathtaking lava arches. Because of yesterday's rainfall, the waterfalls that cascaded down the face of those sheer drops were abundant and spectacular.

Meg felt inconsequential and it made her troubles and challenges fade into the background.

In the shadow of the sacred, she made a vow to not let *thoughts*—especially thoughts about Morgan—bother her, to intrude on this experience.

She vowed the rest of her time here in paradise would just be about full immersion in the sensations that enveloped her.

There would be plenty of time to think after the wedding, once she left Hawaii and *aloha* behind her. For now, she recognized this was the most exquisite gift she could have been given, and she was being asked to embrace it all.

With that vow, she took in the sights and sounds and scents of her friends, the yacht, the ocean and the Napali Coast with an overwhelming sense of delight. She thought the coast and those incredible mountains should be one of the Seven Wonders of the World. It was so stunningly beautiful.

Everyone on board, including the crew, seemed to understand they had been invited to an experience that was rare and compelling.

A kind of quiet reverence—like the deepest of prayers—seemed to infuse everyone on board that vessel.

Midmorning they paused in a beautiful cove and the passengers were invited to swim. There was even a slide from the top deck down into the water!

The quietness they had all experienced seemed to give birth to a kind of exuberance, especially for the men. The guys needed no encouragement, unselfconsciously tossing off their shirts and lining up at the top of the slide, pushing and shoving playfully.

Morgan took his turn. Hands up, head thrown back in laughter, he catapulted down the slide. Maybe she had not even realized how the shadows had become so much a part of him, until that moment when they were completely erased.

Meg felt her love for him, in the joy his happiness made her feel. There was no need to think about tomorrow, she could just relish in his happiness for today.

And her own. She contemplated the delicious feeling inside of her and scrambled up the stairs to the top of the slide.

"It looks like a death spiral," Becky said pensively. She had never been fond of heights. She was the only one who had opted out of the skydiving adventure.

Becky also brought up the possibility of sharks.

There was a delay as Caylee pointed out no one was to get sunburns or strap lines that would spoil the wedding pictures. Sunscreen—provided by a crew that anticipated their every need—had to be applied.

Meg didn't even hesitate to peel off the swim cover and stand there in her bathing suit. If anything, the skimpiness of it made her feel *more* immersed in the experience. She *wanted* the sun and the water to kiss the very same skin Morgan had kissed yesterday. She wanted her body to be baptized by the mountains and the ocean and the very air.

She felt exquisitely, wonderfully, joyously sensual.

So even the potential of sharks and sunburn—and all the other unknown dangers that lurked—could not take that feeling away from Meg. Of being fully alive. Of being determined to delight in whatever gifts were given to her today.

"I'll go first," she said, and stepped up to the top of the slide. Before the other part of her—cautious, adverse to risk—could take over, she plunked herself down and launched.

Becky had been right! It was a death spiral! She was going way too fast, but there was no way to slow herself down.

And so she surrendered, and felt the pure exhilaration of it. She flew off the end of that slide feeling not as if she'd been shot from a cannon, but as though she was able to fly.

The water was gorgeous. Pure and refreshing. It closed over her head. She went down and down and down. And then felt the ocean lifting her back up, as if she was an offering it was spitting out.

When her head popped above the water, she lifted her arms in triumph to the cheering of her friends.

And then the cheering stopped abruptly.

She lowered her arms and scanned the water. Had the dreaded shark been spotted?

Then she saw the item everyone suddenly seemed fixated on.

She squinted at it. What? A jellyfish?

Fear tried to penetrate her sense of euphoria, but it couldn't. Then she saw that tiny, floating black object was even worse than a shark. Or a jellyfish.

Moving on the playful swirl of current created by her splash—and moving right toward Morgan—was her tiny black bikini top.

The strangest thing happened.

She didn't feel embarrassed. At all. In fact, she shouted with laughter.

And then Meg was in very real danger of drowning as she used her hands and arms to cover herself, instead of to keep her head above water. She went under and breathed some water in. She rose, coughing and flailing but still laughing.

And then Morgan was there.

"Hey," he said, getting one shoulder under her arm, and treading water.

Here she was topless in the South Pacific, with all her friends looking on, and her nearly ex-husband rescuing her. It should have been one of the most embarrassing moments of her life.

But it wasn't.

"Hey," she said back, and it felt as if it was just the two of them. And then he was laughing, too.

"Do you have my top?"

He held it up to her like a kid who had captured the flag. And then he wedged his body between her and everyone else. Her exposed breasts were nearly touching him. Of course, she couldn't press against him in front of people!

But he was being so effective in blocking them!

He was just as effective at blocking her, somehow keeping an arm's length between them as he slipped the loop of the bikini strap over her head and behind her neck.

She tugged it into place. When he swam behind her and did up the string knot at the back, the brief touch of his hands was exquisite and intimate, blending beautifully with Meg's decision to enjoy everything.

"I'm doing it up nice and tight."

"Thank you," she said.

"But I'm not sure this *thing* can withstand the slide again. It wasn't exactly made for it."

She glanced over her shoulder, met his eyes, and grinned. She could feel the invitation to be playful—something she had rarely been in her whole life, let alone in the last few months—sparking in the air around them.

"Let's find out," she said. She splashed him in the face, then raced back to the ladder of the yacht. "Last one back down is a rotten egg."

She was only partway up the ladder when his hands circled her waist and he pulled her down and tossed her back into the ocean. He scrambled up the ladder. He was on the second rung when she regained herself and went after him. She got her hands on the waist band of his shorts and pulled.

Hard.

"Hey!" he said, indignant. He reached back with one hand, the other still firmly on the ladder. He tried to yank the fabric from her hands. She held on tight.

"No sense just one of us being exposed," she cackled with delight.

"Full moon on the MeloMelo," Jonathon yelled.

Morgan twisted hard, broke free, but lost his balance and tumbled back into the water. Chortling gleefully, she hefted herself up the ladder and ran across the deck. She raced up the stairs of the yacht, but by the time she was back at the slide, he was right behind her.

She launched herself, arms thrown wide. He hit the water right behind her.

"Best out of three," he called, already nearly to the ladder. Jonathon was part way up it, and turned and gave him a hand. Then shouting like schoolboys, Morgan and Jonathon ran up the sets of steps to the ladder, and came down the slide nearly together.

Everybody was soon infected with the joyous abandon of a game that really didn't have a purpose or a winner or loser. It was just a wild ride to see who could get down the slide and back up to the top of it the fastest. And then come down it the most creatively. People came down the slide in twos, and they came down backwards, they lay flat and they slid on their bellies.

The air rang with squeals and shouts and laughter.

Caught up in it, still in some kind of race with Morgan, though she was pretty sure he had lapped her twice, Meg was at the top of the slide again.

She dived onto it, on her belly, hands extended in front of her. She felt like superwoman flying down that wet, slippery slide.

When she hit the water, she suddenly lost her superpowers. In fact, Meg felt her right arm fold behind her at a strange angle. The pain was instant and immense.

There was an exuberant shout behind her. Meg looked over her shoulder Morgan was flying down it. He was going to land right on top of her!

She was going to die, her pain-filled mind informed her dutifully.

But the part of her that was not dutiful at all, the renegade who had just been released, thought, right through the pain, *But what a way to go.*

CHAPTER FOURTEEN

"MOVE!" MORGAN YELLED at Meg. But, defiantly she didn't. Somehow he managed to grab the sides of the slide just enough to slow himself down. By some miracle, he managed to twist in midair at the last moment so that he didn't crash into Meg.

When he surfaced, he was laughing, but he felt the laughter die when he looked at her face, which was now white with pain. It wasn't playful defiance after all. He swam over to her in two quick strokes.

"What happened?" He wanted to kiss the pain off her face!

"I hit the water wrong," she managed to croak, "I've hurt my shoulder. I can't move my arm."

"Which one?"

"Right."

He looked at her submersed shoulder and felt his heart sink as he peered through the water and saw the weird angle of skin and bone. It was evident to him it was dislocated.

"Your damned curse," he said, softly. "You know there's a sign right at the top of the slide that warns about going down headfirst?"

He used his stern voice to distract her—or maybe himself—as he went over to her uninjured side, getting his shoulder under her arm for the second time today.

"Look, if there's any more rescues, I'll have to start charging you," he said. "I'm not a fireman."

"Oh," she teased, "firemen."

How he missed *this*. Being teased by her.

"What would you charge me?" she said huskily. Even with her in pain *that* was leaping and sizzling in the air between them.

"I'll think about it."

"Okay," she said, a little dreamily. He was pretty sure she was going into shock.

He felt her arm curl around him, the full length of very wet, slippery, nearly naked self press up against his side. But she groaned with pain every single time he moved.

Somehow, inch by torturous inch, he managed to get her to the side of the boat, and then scoop her into his arms and get her up the ladder and on board.

The joyous shouts evaporated as the group realized there had been an accident. Morgan deposited Meg in a lounge chair, and then quickly—like a jealous lover—found a towel to flick over her while the member of the crew who did first aid raced up with the kit and dropped to his knees beside her.

The man looked vaguely familiar.

"Your shoulder is dislocated." He confirmed Morgan's suspicion in an Aussie accent. "I can try and put it back in. It'll hurt like hell, but then the relief will be almost instant."

"Leave it," Morgan said, at the same time Meg said, "Yes, please."

Morgan raced up the deck looking for his clothes, retrieved his cellphone. He was sure he could have a helicopter here in a few minutes. He didn't care what it cost, he was getting her to the hospital.

Then he heard her scream.

He dropped the phone and raced back across the deck.

Meg had her head buried in Caylee's shoulder, sobbing.

"I told you not to," he snapped at the crew member.

"She looked as if she was old enough to make her own decision," he snapped back. Morgan felt an unreasonable desire to punch him in the nose.

"Morgan," Meg told him, backing away from Caylee, "it's good. It's such a relief." Meg lifted her head, smiling through the tears at the first aid guy. "Thank you. I don't know how you knew what to do, Andy."

Andy? When had they come to be on a first-name basis?

"I'm Australian."

Like we couldn't tell from the accent, Morgan thought, but the thought gave him pause. Why, exactly, was he so hostile?

"I worked as a lifeguard at Bondi Beach," Andy said. "Dislocations are one of the most common injuries there."

He seemed to be speaking to Meg alone. She, naturally, beamed at him.

Honestly? An Australian lifeguard? Who had just rescued her from an afternoon of intolerable pain? It was worse than a fireman.

In fact, Andy seemed worse than Magic Mike! And not that he knew anything about those performances, but they did play on women's weaknesses for things like firemen and lifeguards.

Morgan realized, shocked at himself, he was jealous. Well, of course he was jealous! Meg was his wife. She looked unbelievable in that black bathing suit. Okay, the suit was covered with the towel.

But she still looked unbelievable, her wet hair tangled around her face, her green eyes huge, her lips faintly puffy.

Plus, Andy had probably seen her running by at least half a dozen times to get back to the slide.

It occurred to Morgan, current suspicions about Andy having designs on his wife, aside, that he and Meg had been having fun together.

Which he had thought would never happen again.

This hope stirring in him was the worst possible thing! Look at how it was making him react to Andy. As if Meg was *his*.

She lifted her arm experimentally. "It feels tender, but better."

"I think maybe we should turn back," Caylee suggested, but reluctantly. "We'll cut the trip short, and have you checked out by a doctor."

"No! I'm fine now. I wouldn't dream of spoiling the day for everyone else."

"The worst of it is over," Andy said. He went into his first aid kit and pulled out a packet. He took a pen out of his pocket and wrote something on it. He grinned at Meg and handed her the packet. "In Australia, on Bondi, you would have got the famous green whistle to alleviate the pain. The best I can do here is this."

She took the packet. "What is it?"

"Just over-the-counter painkillers and anti-inflammatories. What's that famous line? Take two aspirin and call me."

The saying was actually *Take two aspirin and*

call me in the morning, Morgan thought suspiciously. He glanced at the packet and realized those weren't instructions Andy had written on it. It was his phone number!

"Hey," he growled at Andy, suddenly knowing why he looked familiar, "were you at the shopping village yesterday? During the hula show?"

Andy gave him a baffled look.

Which meant men who found her attractive were coming out of the woodwork! And they all looked the same.

"Right then," Andy said, "I'm going to immobilize it, anyway."

Morgan thought it was very unfair that Australian men just needed to open their mouths and women seemed to find them sexy. He knew that was immature, and he didn't care.

"I'll look after the sling," Morgan said firmly. "I've had first aid training."

Andy stood back and looked at him, and then looked at Meg. Understanding dawned in his eyes.

Morgan wanted to thump on his chest and say *Mr. Hart* and point at her and say *Mrs. Hart*, just so that there were no further misunderstandings on Andy's part.

But Andy seemed to get it completely. He slipped back into purely professional mode as he addressed Meg. "You should take it easy for the rest of the day. If it gives you any trouble, go to the hospital when we dock again."

He searched through his kit and handed Morgan a square of rough white cotton and some safety pins.

Morgan carefully folded the cloth into a triangle, sat on the edge of Meg's chair and gently secured her arm, way too aware of every single thing about her: the droplets of water in her hair, the beads of it on her eyelashes, the salty smell of her skin, the rise and fall of her chest beneath the towel.

He had to resist the impulse to kiss her on the forehead when he was finished. He stood up quickly. Caylee slipped into the place he had been sitting.

She kissed Meg on the cheek. "Maid of honor in a sling. I should have guessed, and adjusted your dress accordingly."

"Well," Meg said, "it might not have been a sling. It might have been crutches. Or a cast on my foot. There's no predicting the direction the curse will take. Or the future."

Caylee's gaze slid to him, and then back to Meg.

"That's true," she said with soft hopefulness. "There's no predicting what will happen next."

"I'll make a prediction," Andy said.

Morgan turned and looked at him. He thought he had gone.

"There won't be any ill effects," Andy said.

"Your accent is making me swoon," Becky said.

Aha! Just as Morgan thought.

Andy grinned cheekily. "By tomorrow, she'll be right as rain. I mean, I wouldn't go zip lining, or outrigger paddling, but she'll be fine for a walk down the aisle holding a posy.

"And another prediction—lunch and then snorkeling at the crater. Except for you, young lady."

He leaned in as if he was going to pat Meg on her naked knee. Morgan wasn't sure if he made a sound like a growl in his throat, or if his look was enough, but Andy managed to resist the touch to the leg, grabbed his kit by the handle and sauntered off whistling.

Lunch, of course, was exquisite, and the mishap didn't seem to change the dynamic of the day. If anything, it seemed to bring the bonds of the groups' friendship into even sharper focus.

After lunch, the boat anchored off Lehua Crater. Morgan didn't want to enjoy the snorkeling when Meg was sidelined, but she insisted he go.

Reluctantly, he listened to the brief lesson on how to use the snorkel, took the camera that was offered him and went into the water with the others.

His sense of astonishment and wonder was

instantaneous. The scene just under the surface of the sea was beyond amazing. Colorful fish— some in huge groups like the yellow ones, and some solitary—swam in and out of a world of coral formations that mirrored the mountain formations above the water.

He took a few pictures, then swam to the ladder, climbed back on the yacht and crouched beside Meg.

"Look at this," he said, scrolling through.

One of the deckhands brought them a laminated card with images of fish on it. Together, Morgan and Meg identified the large school as yellow tangs, a smaller one as convict tangs.

A yellow-and-white-and-black fish with a spectacular fin was a Moorish idol.

Morgan looked at the delight on her face, and had a sudden realization. All this time, had his love for his wife had strings attached?

Unspoken rules?

You must love me back.

You must meet my needs.

He wondered, suddenly, if that was love at all. Wouldn't true love look at the beloved and just genuinely want what was best for them?

Well, maybe not if it involved Andy.

But real love would hold an intention, wouldn't it? That you would always want the best for the other person.

Happiness.

Prosperity.

Peace.

Wouldn't true love require you want that for them, with or without you? Morgan suddenly felt as if he truly understood *aloha*, the spirit of the islands.

It wasn't about getting through the next day and a half with his pride—and his heart—intact. It wasn't about showing her, with a display of wealth like chartering the MeloMelo for a day, what she was missing.

It was about loving her, without strings. Without expectations. Without needing something in return.

Morgan, in that instant, made a vow that he would set aside his personal hurt, pride and feelings and make sure Meg had the best time possible. A gift of pure love to her.

With that in mind, he left her studying the card, jumped back in the water and took more pictures to delight her with. Looking at some extraordinary underwater creature with an eye to sharing his experience with Meg made it, oddly, even more pleasurable.

He loved coming back on deck, sitting beside her on the lounger, water from his hair dripping on her, her uninjured shoulder touching his, as she pored over the photos and then, together they looked them up on the card.

"Look at this one. It's the official state fish of Hawaii," she said, tapping his camera, her eyes round. Then she squinted at the card. "Morgan, look at its name."

He followed her finger to where it was tapping the card. *Humuhumunukunukuapua'a.*

"Say it," she demanded. "Look, the pronunciation is spelled out."

"Hoo-moo-hoo-moo-noo-koo-noo-koo-ah-poo-ah-ah."

She giggled, and then she tried to say it. And then he tried again. And then that damned Andy came along to check on her, glanced at the card, and rattled off the difficult name with annoying ease.

The afternoon melted away as he climbed on and off the boat. And even though sharing with her in this way was fun, Morgan knew if he had to move heaven and earth, he was going to make sure Meg had the real experience someday, too.

The snorkeling portion of the trip came to an end, and the sailboat was moving on. Morgan pulled a deck chair up next to Meg, and let the sun dry the water off his skin.

Though the rest of the group was there, of course, it felt somehow as if he and Meg had formed a unit, with an invisible wall around them.

Connected in a way the others were not. He was aware some tension between them had dissipated.

And been replaced with something even more dangerous. Morgan felt a way with Meg that he had never felt with anyone else on earth.

A deep sense of comfort. Of belonging. Of being at home with her. Of giving her the uncomplicated gift of loving her.

He could not let himself think about where was all that going to go after tomorrow.

He couldn't even let himself think about what it would mean tonight, after they were off the MeloMelo. Would he go back to the bungalow with her?

Good grief, Morgan couldn't believe he was entertaining these kinds of thoughts about Meg. She was wounded! The very thoughts made him aware of how nearly every aspect of his relationship with her was tinged with self-interest.

If he did go back to the bungalow with her, he swore it would be more of *this*. Giving, not receiving. Love without strings attached.

That vow was strangely freeing. It made him feel intensely and purely focused on this moment, as if it was all they had, and all they needed, and nothing—not even tonight and tomorrow—existed outside of this little cocoon of sanctuary they found themselves in.

CHAPTER FIFTEEN

MEG WATCHED AS the sunset stained the sky the most vibrant orange she had ever witnessed. As the MeloMelo pulled back into the bay in front of the Hale Iwa Kai Resort, the ocean, incredibly and impossibly, seemed to be glowing pink.

The group had been served an incredible catch-of-the-day dinner aboard the yacht. By then it had been under sail, instead of using its motor, and the experience of a silent sea and the power in the wind had been as exhilarating as the rest of the day.

In fact, when Meg contemplated her day she was aware of feeling pure bliss. How odd it could feel so perfect, even with her arm in a sling and her shoulder throbbing.

She realized that though the backdrop had been nothing short of spectacular, she could be feeling this same way if she was walking through a dumpster-filled back alley.

It was Morgan at her side that made the world magic.

Something had subtly shifted in him today. She had felt the most exquisite tenderness radiating off of him.

Though it wasn't exactly a new experience—she had felt the same with him before when her curse had played out on their trips together, one of those trips being their honeymoon in Paris.

Morgan just stepped in, did what needed to be done. But he didn't just make things okay, he infused them with his light.

Perhaps it had felt so special today because she had resigned herself to never having that feeling again.

If only, Meg wished wistfully, she had been able to make his world *okay* too. If only she would have been able to infuse his world with the element he most needed: children. Family, and all that meant. Water balloon fights by the lake, little fingers getting burned on marshmallows, the new puppy coming home...all things she had never experienced.

But he had, and he had shared those experiences and memories with her, the longing so strong in his voice it had made her want to give that to him as she had never wanted to give anything to anybody before.

Meg made herself stop this runaway train of thoughts. She would ruin what was left of this perfect day if she indulged in a journey down the road of what she had wanted and could not have.

Instead, she made a conscious effort to just breathe it all in. Her friends were all trying to decide the best way to get her off the sailboat and into the rowboat that would bring them to shore.

"I'm fine," she laughed. "I can do it."

"Let's not risk that, given how I need you slingless tomorrow," Caylee said. Instead of feeling guilty, as if she was a burden, Meg let herself just enjoy *this*.

Her friends caring about her.

Morgan leading the team that was working to tackle the obstacles the world gave them.

Somehow, amid shouts of laughter, Meg found herself in a hammock, being passed carefully from the MeloMelo to the rowboat.

How was she going to live without this? Not just without Morgan, but without all them around her, knowing someone who had your back was always just a breath away?

They let her out of the hammock when she was safely in the rowboat, but they were all there to help her again as they reached shore.

"I can get my feet wet," she protested as Morgan and Jonathon crossed their arms and linked them to make a seat to get her the last few feet to the beach.

It was now nearly completely dark.

Though the shadows, she saw a couple standing there, hand in hand, and she knew who they were even before Caylee squealed.

"Mom, Dad!"

And the perfect day became even more perfect as Caylee's mom hugged Caylee first and then took Meg in her arms, carefully embracing her around the sling.

"My little muffin, what mess have you gotten yourself into now?" she asked, but didn't wait for an answer. "I have missed you so much."

It was homecoming.

This woman, Caylee's mother, had always so generously been her mother, too. It was a sharp and poignant reminder of just how much she had left, how much she had sacrificed, so that Morgan could have the perfect life she dreamed for him.

Mrs. Van Houtte put Meg away from her, and looked at Morgan. "It's good to see you, too, Morgan." And then her gaze went back and forth between the two of them, bewildered and sad, and Meg was afraid she was going to burst into tears or ask, out loud, what every single person had been thinking.

How could this happen to you two when it is apparent you love each other so much?

But she didn't ask it. She bit her lip and returned her attention to Meg.

"Do you want me to look at that? What is it? A dislocation?" Mrs. Van Houtte was a retired nurse.

"No, that's okay," Meg said at the same time Morgan said, "I've got it."

The look Mrs. Van Houtte gave the two of them turned from bewildered to hopeful. She turned to her daughter.

"Caylee," she said. "You're coming with your dad and I. Don't even think you're going to spend the night with Jonathon before your wedding."

"Mom! That's silly, we've been—"

Mrs. Van Houtte held up her hand. "That's between you and your priest, dear. I have only one night left with my little girl before I am the mother of a married woman."

Meg watched them go, and felt that touch of wistfulness she had always felt when she saw how most mothers and daughters were together.

"How's your mom doing?" Morgan asked quietly, watching them go.

He was so in tune with her, and despite the sadness his question made her feel, it intensified her feeling of connection with him.

"She's going through another bad spell. She had been doing pretty good. For a while, I actually thought she might make the wedding."

She laughed—how silly to count on her mother—but heard the undertone of disappointment.

Morgan heard it, too. He put his arm gently around her good shoulder. "I'm sorry, Meggie," he said. "I really am."

"I know," she whispered. He had never, ever acted as if her mother was an embarrassment to him, to a family that had been unsullied by the rollercoaster ride of addiction.

Even though he had never made a judgment, she had probably made enough judgments for both of them.

"Come on," Morgan said, "I'll look after you."

"I can look after myself." That felt like such a lie.

But he gave her the dignity of not challenging it.

Instead, he said mildly, "Well, now that I've promised Mrs. Van Houtte that I'll make sure you're okay tonight. I'm a man of my word, after all."

That was part of the problem.

He was a man of his word, so much so that he would have stayed, even when he knew she couldn't have babies.

Because he was so honorable. But as their friends started having families, would he have regretted his sacrifice? It seemed like it was one of those things that was best not to know.

They walked together back to Huipu. All day, Meg had felt such awareness for Morgan, and of Morgan.

That awareness led her to this realization: it wasn't just about the sex, as incredible as that was between them. It wasn't just about how over-the-top attractive he was.

His masculinity had this other side to it that she could take deep comfort in. Morgan could be counted on, always, to do the right thing.

And tonight, that was just looking after her.

He helped her out of the sling, and then ever so gently, out of the swim cover. He reached around her and undid the knot on the back of her bathing suit, all with about as much feeling as you might expect from a nurse. Then he adjusted the shower, put a towel within her reach, and slid out the door, calling over his shoulder, "Shout if you need help."

Exhaustion from the injury and the active day in the sun was setting in.

She let the warm water from the shower sluice over her, rinsing away the salt water. She stepped out, and grabbed the towel and dried off as best she could one-handed. Then she took another one and tucked it awkwardly around herself.

She padded through to the bedroom. He was in the bed, on top of the covers, pillows propped up behind his shoulders. He looked up from his tablet and leaped from the bed.

"The valet forgot to lay out my pajamas," she teased him.

Teasing Morgan shouldn't feel nearly as good as it did. Homecoming, just like seeing Mrs. Van Houtte had been.

"Failure of duties," he said, with fake contriteness. "What do you want to put on? Pajamas? A T-shirt?"

Both seemed equally unmanageable.

She went over to the bed, pulled back the sheet and slid in between them in the towel. He left the room and came back a few minutes later with water and painkillers.

"Here, take these."

She realized he was as sticky with salt as she had been. Plus, he hadn't changed clothes since yesterday.

"Go shower, Morgan," she said, and he nodded, and went into the closet where his things were and got fresh clothes. Well, that was just as well. There was no telling what would happen if they were both wearing only towels.

Still, it was sweetest torment listening to that water, imagining it sluicing over the hard lines of his body.

By the time he emerged, whatever he had given her for pain was kicking in. She gave him a smile, but she could tell it was distinctly crooked.

He came and sat down on the bed beside her.

"Would you kiss me?" she whispered.

He did. He leaned over and kissed her with exquisite tenderness on her cheek. It wasn't what she expected, and yet, it felt so right.

"How's the pain?" he asked.

"Fading." She actually felt relieved about that platonic kiss, the fact that she could trust him to know what was right in the moment. Somehow, this was just as nice, him beside her, looking at her with tender concern.

"I can tell," he said. "Your eyes are crossing."

"Oh, no!"

"It's kind of cute, like a Siamese cat. Do you want the sling back on?"

"No."

"How are you going to stop yourself from rolling on it in your sleep? We've got you this far. Don't ruin the wedding now."

He was teasing her, and yet, she felt the sting.

"I always ruin everything," she said. "And you always seem to end up like this. Looking after me."

He cocked his head at her, as if she was talking complete nonsense.

"Remember Paris?" she asked.

"I'll never forget Paris," he said softly. "We

might not have had the wedding of your dreams, but we had that."

"What do you mean about the wedding of my dreams?"

"It wasn't like this," he said quietly. "A beautiful location. A wedding party. A gown. A special day for you to feel like a princess."

"We agreed about the wedding," she said, puzzled. "It was what suited both of us."

"So you say," he said dubiously. "Aren't you sorry we didn't have this? Just a little bit?"

"No," she said. "We had Paris to make up for it."

"See?" he said triumphantly. "There was something you lacked, that you needed making up for."

"Morgan! That's not true."

He looked so unconvinced, that Meg wanted to remind him of that special, special time.

"What was your favorite thing?" she asked.

Despite how brotherly he was being at the moment, the look he gave her was white-hot.

She gulped and felt heat rising in her cheeks. "Besides that?"

He didn't even hesitate. He didn't say the Louvre or the Eiffel Tower or the Arc de Triomphe.

"We'd been walking all day and into the night. We'd squeezed so much sightseeing into our first two days. Then, we stopped at that little café overlooking the Seine as the sun was setting. It was on a cobblestone street and we sat outside under a pink awning."

"We ordered hot chocolate," she remembered, "and they brought us heated milk with pots of chocolate on the side."

"And the waiter brought us an éclair, on the house, to share. It felt as if the whole world knew we were madly in love and everyone was celebrating with us."

"Everything seemed to shine," she recalled softly, "as if it was lit from within."

They were silent for a moment.

"And then I ruined it all. Just like I said. I always ruin everything."

He looked genuinely surprised. "Is that how you see it?"

"Of course. That's how it was. Five minutes after we finished that hot chocolate and the éclair, I tripped on that loose cobblestone. Snap. The romance of Paris traded for a ride in an ambulance and the bright lights and chaos of an emergency room." Meg sighed heavily, remembering. "Honestly? I didn't expect to test for better or worse quite so soon."

"I never saw it like that," he said quietly.

"How else was there to see it?"

"I felt as if we saw a side of Paris others don't get to see."

"The inside of an emergency room?"

"The old grandma, in her lovely pink beret, and her jewels, with her family surrounding her. Even though I don't speak French, you could tell every word they said to her was loving her into the next life. They cherished her, and she knew it."

Meg's eyes sparked with tears. A man who saw *this*.

"That little boy," he continued softly, "clutching the teddy bear, his mother soothing him. Again, you didn't have to speak French to know the universal language."

Of course, he would see the little boy. With longing for a little boy of his own one day, no doubt.

Still...

"I never knew you saw it like that," Meg whispered.

"When I was with you, I saw the best in everything, I guess, even in what you saw as the worst."

She felt as if she was holding back tears.

"I liked looking after you, Meg," he told her softly. "It never felt like it was a burden. I should have made sure you knew that sooner."

The tears were still threatening. She tried to hold them off with good, healthy skepticism.

"Even when I got food poisoning in Thailand? I was in the bathroom for three days. Our whole holiday, practically. And you barely left my side. Just to go in search of ginger ale."

"Not an easy item to find in Thailand," he agreed, but with astounding affection. "I had to go to a bar in a hotel where Canadians hung out. Three blocks, in that grueling heat, at a dead run."

"At least a dozen times," she reminded him.

"At least," he said with a fond smile.

"Switzerland," she reminded him, "We went out on that boat on Lake Geneva. And I just wanted to look gorgeous for you, and I didn't dress warm enough, and the next thing you knew..."

"The best part," he said. "Crawling into the hospital bed beside you, your ice-cold body next to mine, under the sheets with a heating pad, feeling you coming back to life."

The love she felt for him was suddenly so intense, more intense, even, than after they had made love.

The pills seemed to be working.

"Meg," Morgan said, "even though it never bothered me, what do you think it was about? The curse?"

"Bryan." She shocked herself by saying it. What part of her subconscious were the drugs unleashing?

"What? Your brother?"

"I loved him," she said. "I loved him madly."

"Of course you did."

"But—"

She fell silent. She had never said this to a living soul.

"But?" Morgan's voice was so soft. She looked deeply at him. The man she could say anything to. And yet she had never said this.

"Everything was about him, Morgan. I remember once Mrs. Van Houtte and Caylee asked me to go to a movie with them. You know what I did? I asked if I could have the money instead. I'm embarrassed thinking about it, but Bryan needed a new wheelchair. Of course, Mrs. Van Houtte gave me the money, and then some.

"I remember my mom kissing me and calling me a saint when I gave her that money. I felt so approved of. Sometimes I feel like the only time my mom acknowledged I existed was when I did something for Bryan.

"I babysat all summer and gave the money to Mom? That was wonderful! I didn't join school clubs, because that cost money? What a beautiful soul I had. I didn't need a new winter jacket this year? What a trooper! Bryan got a new winter jacket, of course, because we wouldn't want Bryan to catch a cold."

Meg heard Morgan's sharp intake of breath, and felt guilty for saying these things. But she'd started and now it felt as if she was compelled to finish.

"And then I got the scholarship for art camp! I was going away, I was going to the one place where I could lose myself, where I could be free of all the reoccurring drama and trauma at home. Art! The one place I got recognized for me, where it wasn't all about my brother. And what happens when I did something for myself? The hammer of fate dropped on my head. Bryan died while I was away."

"Meg, I'm so sorry," Morgan said gruffly.

She sighed. "And did my mom turn all that love and affection she'd lavished on Bryan onto me, her grieving daughter? No, she did not. It became all about her. Maybe it always had been. I think soaking up all that attention and sympathy made her feel special in ways I could not.

"I think my mom was totally addicted to Bryan and when he was gone, she turned that addictive personality on to something else.

"That's why I have the curse," she finished, with a dangerous hiccup. "I'm scared to have fun. No, I punish myself for having fun."

"You never said any of this before," Morgan said, drawing her head onto his chest.

She let the tears flow. "Because I never wanted you to know what kind of person I really am. Resentful of my brother and my mom."

"Oh, Meggie," he said softly, and she wept at the acceptance she heard in his voice. It occurred to her she might tell him. Her deepest secret. About the one thing she could not give him.

But then, instead, with his hand in hers, her eyes shut and she floated off feeling safe and loved and protected in a way she had not in eight months.

When she woke up in the morning, Morgan was gone. Meg waited for a feeling of guilt about revealing the things she had to hit her, but it did not. Instead the sensation was one of bliss—of being loved by a man like Morgan even when he knew everything there was to know about her.

Well, almost everything.

There was a note next to the bed.

Not a love note. A stern warning to use the sling. She remembered today was the day Caylee and Jonathon were getting married.

For Meg, that feeling that had begun on the boat—of being part of something bigger, of being accepted into the tribe, of being loved—only intensified as the day unfolded.

Her right shoulder was quite a bit better. Tender, and bruised, but it was in no way debilitating. Still, she put on the sling, just to make sure she was at her best for the ceremony.

For some reason—maybe it was the crate of wedding clothes that had been delivered while they were on the yacht, maybe they all carried the beauty of the day on the MeloMelo inside of them, maybe it was *aloha*—but the feeling of bliss grew and grew and grew as the ceremony drew closer.

No one was frazzled.

There were no arguments.

There were no upsets about last-minute details.

Even the unpredictable Kauai weather seemed intent on cooperating.

The day started with the women gathered under a shade shelter, with a palm-frond roof. Tables were laden with flowers and leaves.

Local women had come to show them how to make leis for the guests and the bridal party. The first leis were made with the gloriously scented purple-and-white plumeria. The scent of the flowers intermingled with a smell of burning wood drifting up from the beach.

At Mrs. Van Houtte's insistence, Meg's arm was still in a sling.

"Right up until the ceremony," Mrs. Van Houtte

told her with a stern shake of her finger. It felt good to be mothered.

At first, Meg didn't know if she would be of any help, but a job was found for her—sorting through the huge baskets of flowers and choosing only the perfect, unflawed blossoms.

As she sorted, one of the local women began to speak. "The wedding luau feast is being prepared. That's the burning smell. The resort has a permanent pit for events like this, so it didn't have to be dug.

"The wood and rocks were put in it early, early this morning. When the wood has burned down, it will be removed, and a whole pig will be put on top of the hot rocks, then wrapped in banana leaves. It will slowly cook and steam all day. The first slow cooker!"

A bridal lei of orchids was made for Caylee to wear around her neck. After that, satisfied perhaps that the visitors to the island had a basic grasp of the work, they were shown how to make the white *haku lei*—the Hawaiian flower crown—that Caylee would wear.

For the men, they made ti leaf maile-style leis. Rather than a circle, it was a long line of leaves with a few flowers braided into it that the groom and his groomsmen would wear over their shoulders, a bit like the vestments of a priest.

For Meg, the beauty of working with the

women was astonishing. The tropical breezes embraced them, and the view of a turquoise ocean was stunning.

But it was being with this circle of women that made her heart feel as if it was glowing like the warm rocks that were now cooking the pig, the scents of the meat beginning to hang tantalizingly in the air.

The shelter was filled with the murmur of quiet voices, the occasional laugh or giggle, the fragrance of the flowers.

Stories were told. And songs were hummed. Chants were taught. Prayers were murmured.

Meg realized she loved the traditional feel of the women gathering in the shaded structure. It felt as if there were no differences between them. The barriers of different ages, cultures, physical appearances, faded away as they worked together toward doing what women do, creating. They became one, weaving the ancient secrets of feminine energy into these wedding adornments.

As their fingers moved, it felt as if blessings were being sewn in: the celebration of love, the age-old dreams that could be fulfilled when a couple chose to walk through life together, how their choice to join brought the future into sharp focus.

As the morning progressed, Meg was aware of a kind of bittersweetness overcoming her.

Because, at its very heart, a wedding was a vow to the future.

I will send my children and my grandchildren forward to a time I will never see.

So, while it was a wonder to be included in this women's day, Meg also acutely felt her lack. Her barrenness. The fact that she could not fulfill what her wedding had promised.

All through the morning, Meg was aware of the men working toward the same goal, the making of a perfect celebration of love, but separately from them.

She strained to catch glimpses of Morgan. Every time she saw him, or heard him, her heart did this trill of recognition, like a bird singing.

She longed to be with him, but was so aware it was the longing of the damned. A kind of desperate need to see Morgan, to fill her senses with him, before she found the courage to say goodbye to him once again.

So that he could someday realize everything that a day like this stood for.

The continuation of the life cycle, the perpetuation of the generations.

After they had finished with the leis, they went to the spa to have their hair and makeup done.

And then, finally, they slipped into their dresses. Caylee looked so stunningly beautiful that they all wept and then had to have their makeup repaired.

Meg was finally allowed to remove her sling. She needed help getting dressed. The bruise around her shoulder was spectacular and they were all thankful that her dress had a short cap sleeve on it that hid the worst of that discoloration.

It felt like a dream as Meg waited for her turn to walk down the aisle that had been created on the beach.

Chairs with tropical flowers on the backs of them had been set up on a newly constructed wooden platform. The seating faced the ocean and a shade arbor, the side and top of which were woven with more beautiful flowers.

The guests, each who had been greeted with a lei, were now seated.

The groom and his groomsmen waited under the arbor, the ti leaf maile leis dark against the whiteness of their shirts and suits.

Morgan was standing at Jonathon's shoulder. Meg had waited all day to fill her senses with him, and the moment did not disappoint.

Looking at Morgan filled her with a poignant delight. He looked tanned and relaxed, and so, so handsome it took Meg's breath away. When he looked at her, she saw a look on his face that every single woman lives to see.

That he cherished her.

That he would protect her with his own life if needs be.

She would not spoil one second of what was left of this day by thinking of tomorrow. Not one. Instead, she would give herself over to the magic that was unfolding around them.

A single ukulele began to strum, not the traditional wedding march, but instead "It's A Wonderful World."

Samantha went first, then Becky, then Allie.

And then Meg was walking down the aisle, and it felt as if this was only about her and Morgan, her walking toward him, as his eyes fastened on her, wistful and reverent as any groom.

When Caylee came on her father's arm, Meg was finally able to drag her eyes from Morgan's.

The bride was stunning, but even the glory of that dress paled in comparison to the look on Caylee's face, a radiance spun out of pure love. She reached Jonathon, and Meg took her bouquet.

The bride and the groom exchanged those age-old vows.

For better or for worse.

In sickness and in health.

Meg had said those words. Hearing them again, for the first time since she had left Morgan, she allowed herself the luxury of doubt.

She had made that vow to him. He had made his to her.

And she had broken hers.

For the best possible reason, and yet…

She couldn't. Not today, she couldn't doubt herself. She would just give herself over to what time she had left.

Doubts were for after.

Doubts, regrets, were for the rest of her life.

Not for this magical day.

At the end of the ceremony, Jonathon slipped the ti leaf maile lei from around his neck, and placed it on Caylee's. She took off her orchid lei and put it around his neck.

And then, they kissed.

And it was so much more than a kiss. A fusion. A bond. A promise.

The future shimmering between them like an enchantment.

After the wedding party signed the register, Caylee and Jonathon went down the aisle, and the spectators showered them in flower petals.

Meg and Morgan joined hands and followed. The walk through the rain of petals, with his hand warm in hers, invited her to journey into the world of enchantment that the kiss between the bride and groom had begun.

"How's your shoulder?" Morgan asked, quietly.

Always *this*. The tenderness, the concern, the

sense he gave her of being protected and cherished.

Loved.

Just the way she loved him.

Meg considered this: Had she broken her vow to him when she left him, or had she kept it? Had she been true to it, by putting his needs ahead of her own?

He touched her forehead.

"Not today," he said gently. "Let's not worry today."

"Okay," she agreed, and smiled up at him. That felt like a vow.

And she gave herself over to that vow completely. She left her worries behind and immersed herself in the activities of the day, beginning with the photo session.

There were traditional photos, with the spectacular backdrop of the ocean and the mountains.

The photographer was wonderful, giving them tips on how to look natural, but to Meg, it felt as if it was Morgan who coaxed the best out of her. Teasing her, cajoling her, reaching over to rearrange a single strand of hair, removing an imaginary smudge from her lip with his thumb.

After the more traditional shots, the photographer encouraged the men to take off the jackets and to let loose, so there were playful photos, too. Jonathon shinnying up a palm tree and dropping a coconut to his bride; Morgan and Meg running along the edge of the sand, barefoot, shrieking with laughter; the women wading out into the white froth of the surf, holding up their dresses and bouquets.

The entire day was simply infused with that energy of enchantment. All things were touched by it, from the preparations that morning to the ceremony, to the photos to the unearthing of the pig and now the luau in full swing.

Besides her own wedding day, and despite her shoulder trying to remind her she really was cursed, Meg decided this was easily the best day of her life.

She refused to look at the goodbye looming like storm clouds on the horizon.

CHAPTER SIXTEEN

MORGAN HAD NEVER been to a wedding quite like this one. As well as the unbridled joy, there was an unexpected sensuality shimmering in the air around the entire day.

But, of course, it was Hawaii, that deeply ancient, mysterious and sensual land.

And of course it was in the looks and touches that passed between Caylee and Jonathon, so unconsciously loaded with passion and intimacy that surely it was creating this sense of deep longing in everyone, not just him?

But, perhaps most of all, it was in just being with Meg.

It was remembering all they had been to each other, but experiencing her anew, also. It felt as if some part of him that was essential had been restored to him, some part broken was repaired.

And the feeling just built as the day went on.

Of a connection so strong it felt sacred and unbreakable. It felt as if no man—and no woman—could possibly stop it, not any more than they could have stopped that storm that had literally swept them back into each other's arms.

The dancing had begun and now, under a dark tropical sky, with the lap of the waves a backdrop to the music, they were in each other's arms. Well, arm. Because Meg had her sling back on, and her one arm was sandwiched between them as they swayed together and he gazed into her eyes, thinking, *It will never be enough.*

Even a lifetime with her, and it will not feel like I've had enough of her.

Her scent filled him, her body felt exquisitely right against his, the look in her eyes was something every man lived for.

The stars had long since come out. Even the chickens had gone to bed. And yet no one wanted to say goodbye to this day.

The dancing continued until well past one in the morning. It might have gone on until dawn, except that Kauai decided to show them who was in charge, and it was not mere mortals.

It began to rain, gently at first, and then harder. When it began to pelt down, the band gave up and hastily packed up their equipment. The staff scurried to get food off the table that had been set up for snacks hours ago.

And then, without any discussion, he had Meg's good hand in his, and they were running, laughing, along one of the paved paths.

At the last minute, though, he did not turn toward Huipu.

Morgan wanted to show her what he had found on his first day here, before she had arrived.

He took her down a paved path, the torches sputtering in the pouring rain. They came to a subtle signpost. An arrow pointed toward Lover's Grove.

On that sign was a placard that read Unoccupied.

He turned it over. *Occupied*. A simple system, a guarantee of privacy for lovers who came here.

The path wound through a jungle of lush thick greenery into a little grotto. A turquoise pool, lit so that the water danced as if it was living, was surrounded by growth, leathery green leaves, flowers, delicate ferns. At one end of it, a manmade waterfall cascaded down. Under that tumbling water was a cave.

From the first moment he had seen this place, Morgan had been stunned at how clearly he could see himself here.

With the woman who had abandoned him.

And broken his heart.

Even when he had woken, that first night, to find Meg standing beside the bed, this is where he had pictured her.

The next morning, he had felt as if it was his

mission—if he wanted to protect himself—to keep her away from this place.

But all his efforts now felt ridiculously puny in the face of what was between them. He had been clearly shown that when the flash flood had driven them into that shelter.

That at close proximity he was powerless against her.

Now, this place, Lover's Grove, felt as if it had been a premonition. As if he had known, all along, they would end up here.

And that somehow, what happened between them here would make everything that had gone wrong between them right again.

Tenderly, he reached for her.

Tenderly, he took her in his arms.

Tenderly, he removed her sodden dress, kissed the raindrops from her lifted face, and then from the other soaked, perfect surfaces of her skin.

And then his own clothes followed hers to that heap of sopping cloth as their feet.

Morgan took Meg in his arms, and did what this entire day, this entire time here in Hawaii, had been calling him to do.

He claimed his wife back. He laid his poor battered, bruised, damaged heart at her feet. He told her with his lips and his touch, and his tongue and with his gaze, the truth that laid him bare to her, that opened his chest to her sword, should she choose to use it.

He told her, without words, but with every other tool at his disposal, that he loved her.

And that he always would.

To his dying breath.

This had been building between them, Meg thought with wonder, as surely as the storm that had let loose all around them.

She had never seen a place like this secret little grotto. She had never been in a place that felt so perfect.

To answer the calling of her body to his.

Her lips to his.

To answer the calling to be Morgan's wife. One more time.

On the last occasion that they had made love, there had been an undeniable fury to it, a repressed urgency, a pent-up need that had to be satiated *right then*.

This time was totally different.

Maybe partly because the recent injury to her shoulder, though that just felt, to her, like part of it.

The injury was the world giving them the *shaka*: telling them to slow down, hang loose, take it easy, everything's fine.

Oh, no, so much more than fine, Meg thought,

as Morgan lifted the hem of her sodden dress, and she raised her arms to help him. Even the pain of that effort on her injured shoulder felt oddly delicious as he dropped the dress away, helped her lower her arm, placed kisses that felt as if they had the power to heal any wound all over that bruise.

Just like her, he seemed to feel the whispering—*Slow down. You have all the time in the world.*

He explored her with heart-melting tenderness. She felt the wonder that she had chosen this man to be her husband, the only person in the world who knew her in this way.

The only person in the world who would ever know her in this way.

Of course, she knew what was not true was that they had all the time in the world. That knowledge, tucked away in some dark corner of her mind, made *this* even more exquisite, achingly poignant, terrifyingly tender. Because she knew she could never give herself in this way to another person. Not ever. Not if she lived to be in her hundreds.

So, this was it for her, before she entered a world of self-imposed chastity, a world that would not have Morgan coaxing a side of her to the surface that she had never known before him.

And would never know again, after.

She slipped his clothes from him with all the

exquisite tenderness that he had shown her. She drew him into the turquoise water, and then into the waterfall.

With the warm water tumbling around them, joining the rain, wet on wet, she tilted her head and he dropped his mouth over hers.

His kiss was lingering and sweet, as was her answer. She explored the jagged edge of his front teeth with her tongue, the swell of his top lip.

They moved past the tumble of water into the cave behind it. It felt like a secret place, entirely removed from all the world. The walls reflected dancing light from the water, and that light danced off their faces, too.

She explored his face, and then every silky inch of him with excruciating slowness. First, she let her fingertips commit his body to her memory, and then she made sure to burn it in, forever, by following that trail laid by her fingertips with her tongue.

And then Morgan stilled her quest, and their positions reversed. He became the explorer as he kissed droplets of water off her lashes, nibbled her earlobes, claimed her mouth, trailed fire down her water-slick body.

She noticed he was trembling with leashed desire. She realized she was, too. And still, by some silent agreement, it was a slow cherishing.

His lips returned to her mouth, and he tasted,

and tasted and tasted, as if her mouth was a delicacy he could never get enough of. His tongue ran over her lips, already puffy from kissing, then darting into the hollow of her mouth and back out. He nibbled her lips with his teeth, drew them into his mouth, sucked on them gently, plundered her mouth with his tongue again.

And all the while that his mouth held hers captive, his hands roamed her with the same slow tenderness.

Morgan did what he had always done to her.

In this secret place, he brought her to her secret place. He exposed things about her that only Morgan knew. What he knew was that Meg, just below the surface, was erotic and sensual. Her secret was that she was hungry. Her secret was that she was desperate for every stroke of his hands laying claim to her.

His touch awakened her. Her breasts, her belly, between her legs, her very skin screamed its wanting of him, its insatiable need for him.

And yet, still, as the water cascaded down around them, he held back, stoking the fire, hotter and hotter, pulling back and letting it cool, only to stoke again.

His lips and his hands were the fuel to her flame. He knew it. He played it. Only when she was sobbing with wanting and need did he back her up against the wall of the cave. He lifted her with such easy strength, lifted her to him, guided her legs to wrap around the power of his torso.

It was, to this point, as if they had been swimming against a current, and suddenly let go.

To the bliss of pure surrender.

His eyes never leaving hers, he claimed her, the bliss building and building and building until it was something else entirely, until it felt as if they stood on the edge of a cliff ready to plummet to their deaths.

A scream formed on her lips when they fell toward their destiny, but he covered her mouth with his, and took the scream from her.

And they did not plummet.

They flew.

They joined the pounding of the rain and of the waterfall, they joined the blackness of the sky, and the cry of the wind.

In that explosive crescendo they became everything.

And everything became them.

This moment, this mystical moment between a man and his wife, had been written long before they were born.

It was what the mountains around them bore silent witness to, what the women had woven into the leis, what had underscored the humming and the chants.

This was a land of ancient knowledge.

And it called for them to know.

To know each other completely.

To become a part of all of it.

To embrace the darkest unknown secrets a heart could hold, until they were the secret, to sink into the great mystery until they were the mystery, to honor the forces of creation until they became creation itself.

Complete, with the stars and the water and the mountains swirling around them and in them, Morgan lifted her.

He walked out of the pool. Now she noticed there were two deep lounge chairs here and there were stacks of white towels on a rack. It was a bit jarring to realize that they were not really in a secret grotto.

Morgan, ever so tenderly, set her on her feet, and tucked a towel around her, and then one around himself.

With the rain still pouring down around them, they gathered up the soaked piles of clothes, and ran, clad only in their towels, barefoot and laughing back to Huipu.

He laid her across the bed and came on top of her, traced the line of her lips with his thumb.

And then he said it.

"I love you."

She knew she should not say it. That it would

only make the farewell worse when that time came, and that time was coming soon.

But she could no more have stopped the words from coming out than she could stop the rain from falling down.

"I love you," she whispered in return.

And in the half light, she traced the line of his nose and his lips with her fingertips, drank in his moonlight-drenched face, memorizing every glorious detail of him.

"Don't ever leave me again, Meg." His voice was hoarse with pain, his need laid unvarnished before her.

She saw her silence register in his eyes. She saw he was stunned by it, and then he pushed himself off the bed, gave her one look of betrayed astonishment and was gone into the night.

Meg wept.

CHAPTER SEVENTEEN

MORGAN STEPPED BACK out into the night and felt a war of conflicting emotions. The rain had stopped, though he could hear water dripping off the nearby foliage.

He felt the fullness in his heart. Tenderness. Love.

He loved Meg. He was never going to stop. And yet, nothing was resolved between them.

He had done tonight what he did not want to do.

He had begged her. *Don't ever leave me again, Meg.*

Had Meg rewarded his vulnerability with an assurance? A promise? A commitment?

No, she had not.

Her silence had spoken for her.

For all that they had given in to the enchantment around them today, for all that the love in the air—*aloha*—had melted every one of their barriers, now Morgan felt unsettled and uncertain.

How could it have been a good thing to let

Meg back in, when they had not discussed where were they going next? In three more days, would she simply go back to the life she had found?

Without him?

He was tempted to go back and demand answers, and yet he was not sure he could handle what those answers were. He had seen something terrifying in her expression when he had begged her not to leave him.

Begged.

In his defense, it had come on the heels of an entire day that could only be called blissful. He glanced at his watch.

It was nearly 3:00 a.m.

The perfect day was over. The new one was already unfolding. Soon, the damned chickens would be cheering on the sunrise.

Restlessly, he walked down the dark pathway through the quiet resort to the ocean. It was gorgeous in the moonlight, and without hesitation he went into the water and swam.

He told himself he was giving in to the water, but he knew the residue of uncertainty remained.

When he stepped back onto the sand, he was no longer alone on the beach.

Caylee was sitting there, still in her wedding dress, looking like a dream of a princess out of a fairy tale. If he had his phone with him, he would be tempted to snap a picture. If he shared it with Meg, she might paint it.

But again, everything was so nebulous between them. How much would they be sharing?

He walked over to Caylee, and she patted the sand beside her. He sank into it.

"The bride alone on her wedding night?" he asked.

"Not in a bad way," she said. "Jonathon's fast asleep. I somehow can't let go of it. The day. The vows. The perfection. The joy. It's singing inside of me, and it's not ready to stop yet."

"Every single person felt that, Caylee. Your wedding was a gift from you and Jonathon to each of us who shared the day with you."

It was true. Morgan was not sure he had ever experienced a more wonderful and amazing day. The wedding had been exactly what every bride dreams of, perfect, blissful, magical.

That enchantment had gotten all over everyone. *That* was how he was going to explain what had happened between him and Meg, again. A spell they were under.

And underneath that, awareness of the enormity of it all.

"We're going to have babies together," Caylee whispered, her arms wrapped around her knees as she gazed out at the ocean.

He slid her a look. "You're pregnant?"

She gave him a playful slug on his shoulder, a lovely little familiarity, the kind close friends enjoy.

"Morgan! I meant *someday* Jonathon and I will have children. We're going to be adults."

He and Meg had shared that dream. But he realized adults didn't get to claim they had been under a spell rather than taking responsibility for their actions.

It also occurred to him he had not given a single thought to taking precautions with Meg, which also seemed irresponsible given how up in the air things were between them. On the other hand, he felt this sense of delicious wonder when he thought of Meg having their baby.

"Things seem good between you and Meg," Caylee offered, as if she knew his thoughts had turned to Meg. Her voice was soft with hope.

He sighed, took up a fistful of sand and then let it sift out between his fingertips.

"*Are* things going to be okay between you?" Caylee pressed.

He looked at her and then looked away. "I'd be able to answer that better if I understood what had happened the first time. When she left. Did she tell you? Did she confide in you? Anything beyond what she told me? That she couldn't handle the lifestyle?"

"That's exactly what she told me. I never believed her, though."

"Me either."

"I never pressed her, Morgan. I've known Meg so long. I've known her since we were little kids. I trusted whatever reasons she had, they came from that good, good heart of hers."

"Sure," he said cynically.

"It's true."

"Meg seemed so happy married to me," Morgan said pensively. "But last night she told me some things that made me realize she's wary of happiness."

He realized, just saying that, it was a failing on his part that Meg had not told him those things sooner.

Caylee drew in a long breath and slid him a look.

"It's not just happiness," she said pensively, after a long silence. "You know, us girls have our crazy adventure club. We've been rock climbing and white water rafting and horseback riding. Not a single scratch on her. Not one visit to the hospital. No famous travel curse when she was with us. But even yesterday, there it was. Like she was just having way too much fun *with you*."

Morgan drew in a breath. "What are you saying?"

"It's love," Caylee said quietly. "I think Meg

is manifesting her deepest belief. That love is gonna hurt. That she doesn't deserve it. That she'll be punished for every moment of happiness that she steals from the jaws of fate."

Caylee was silent again. She wouldn't look at him.

He felt as if he was going to stop breathing as he realized the truth.

"You know," he whispered. "You know why she left me."

"I'm only guessing."

"Please tell me what you think."

Caylee wrapped her arms tighter around her knees, drew them in closer to her chest.

"She left all of us," she confided softly. "You know what that made me think, when she cut herself off from everybody? That she had a secret she didn't want to tell, that she was going to carry all by herself, that good little soldier she was raised to be. She didn't want to be around us because we would have loved her secret out of her, and she knew it."

"What secret?" he asked, hoarsely. "Was there someone else?"

Caylee shot him a look loaded with scorn. "Do you know her at all?"

"I thought so," he said defensively.

The awful thought that maybe she was sick crossed his mind. It was everything he could do not to leap up right this second, go to her and look at her for signs. She did look like she'd lost weight, those new hollows under her cheekbones, the jut of her shoulders…

"She never told me," Caylee said, drawing patterns in the sand with her hand, letting her hair fall in front of her face so he couldn't read her expression.

He wasn't having it. He nudged her with his shoulder and when she looked up he saw the sorrow in her eyes.

"Tell me what you think," he said.

He'd never, ever been a pushy kind of guy, but he heard the demand in his voice.

Caylee nodded.

"I think she thought she could have a baby like Bryan. That it was genetic. I always wondered if she'd been tested. You know, they can discover all kinds of things with genetic testing these days."

Morgan went very still. Meg had, after all, just revealed to him how her whole life had revolved around her brother.

Was it possible that she was terrified of her life revolving around a child with disabilities?

They'd been trying so hard to have a baby. They'd been just like Jonathon and Caylee, so ready for the next step in their lives. But when he thought back on it, Meg had been way more invested in it than him. He'd just thought it would happen when the time was right.

And then, one day, he recalled, she seemed to lose interest.

And not long after that, he had found the note.

He wished he felt compassion for her as he got up off the sand. He didn't even say goodbye to Caylee. He strode back toward their bungalow.

But he didn't feel compassion at all.

He felt fury. Because they would have weathered anything they faced together. But he had not even been consulted. Or trusted. The fact was, Meg had not thought he would honor those words he had spoken to her on their wedding day.

Meg wiped away the tears. She knew she had to leave and she had to leave right now. It didn't matter that it was the middle of the night.

She had been greedy. She had stolen more time with him.

Ultimately, she had been so selfish. Because she had hurt Morgan even more. She couldn't be here when he got back.

She couldn't.

Because if he asked her that one more time— *Don't ever leave me again, Meg*—she would not be able to do it. She would not be able to do what she knew he needed her to do to have the life he so desperately wanted and that he so deserved to have.

She tumbled from the bed, found her suitcase, began to throw things in it, her movements fraught with a sense of urgency.

But she was not quick enough. She heard the door open and she whirled to face Morgan, steeling herself to be stronger than she had ever been before.

Meg stared at her husband. He'd been in the ocean. He was shirtless, his skin had the faint sheen of salt on it. His hair was curly and damp. His beautiful, perfect male body was illuminated in moonlight.

And yet, he looked like a stranger. She had never seen that expression on his face before. She had never seen him angry before. Oh, sure. Irritated. Annoyed. Frustrated.

But nothing like this. His eyes were snapping with fury, his expression was grim, his mouth was a slashing frown.

He was not the same man who had held her so tenderly not even an hour ago. He was not the man who had left here. He was not a man about to beg her to change her mind.

CHAPTER EIGHTEEN

"IT'S FOR BETTER or worse," Morgan said, his voice harsh.

"Wh-wh-what?" Meg stammered.

"I know why you really left," he told her, and she felt everything in her go cold.

"I don't know what you mean."

"Can't handle the lifestyle, my ass."

"Okay," she said. She stopped putting things in the suitcase. She went and sat on the edge of the bed. She braced herself for the fact that somehow he had found out the truth. She braced herself against the rage pouring off of him.

"Tell me why I really left," she whispered.

"You had some kind of test done. You thought you carried the gene. For what Bryan had. And you didn't trust me with it. You didn't trust me to be man enough to live up to those words, for better or worse."

"You're wrong," she said quietly. "It didn't have anything to do with Bryan."

The wind went out of his sails. He collapsed,

then sat on the edge of the bed beside her, but not touching her.

"Just tell me the damned reason, Meg. Tell me! You're killing me, do you get that? Especially after the last few days. If you leave me again, I won't make it."

"But you will," she said softly. "We both know that. That people can survive what seems unsurvivable."

"But you're not dead," he spat at her. "You're alive. I can't function on this planet knowing you're alive somewhere and you don't want to be with me."

The torment on his face collapsed every wall she had built against this very moment.

She moved beside him, guided his head to her shoulder, ran her fingertips through his beautiful, damp, salty sand-colored curls.

"I can't have babies," she whispered. "That's why I left."

For a moment, he froze, and then he leaped away from her touch and off of the bed. He turned back to her, looking down at her, his fists clenching and unclenching.

"That's why you left?" There was something dangerous in his tone.

"Yes," she said.

He stared at her, his eyebrows arrowed down, his eyes flashing with disdain.

"That's even *worse*," he told her, the quietness of his tone accentuating his fury, rather than dissipating it. "You couldn't trust me with that? As if you're the only adult in the room? You're the only one who can handle it?"

She took a deep breath, and closed her eyes.

"I've seen how you pined for your family, Morgan," she finally said, when she felt she was composed enough to say it without crying. "For your brother and your sister-in-law, but especially for the children, for Kendra and James.

"I've seen how your eyes follow children playing with this world-weary sorrow in them. I knew what it would take to make your heart whole again, and when I found out I couldn't give it to you, I backed away. So that you could find what you needed with someone else."

His mouth fell open. The fury didn't lessen in his eyes. It deepened. "That's why you fixated on Marjorie and what you perceived as her lack of interest in children."

"Yes," she confessed, her voice a whisper.

"Thank you, Saint Meg," he said, his tone so caustic it felt as if it could flay the skin off her bones. "Thank you for knowing the miracle I needed, and even the kind of woman I needed to achieve it. I'm surprised you didn't set up interviews for your replacement! Maybe she could have provided a doctor's certificate proving fertility.

"Thank you for knowing everything I needed in life before I knew it myself.

"Thank you for breaking my heart, for nearly killing me with grief and self-doubt, but all for my own good, of course."

"Morgan, please don't make what I did ugly."

"I don't have to make it ugly," he said. "You did that. I'm just naming it."

She wanted to get up and run from the disdain pouring off of him, but she made herself sit still.

"Thank you for not looking at a single option," Morgan spat out. "Are there medical things we could have done? What about adoption? For God's sake, lots of people our age just get dogs."

"Right," she said, holding her hands together so he could not see the shaking. "You would have been happy with puppies instead of children."

"I would have been happy with *you*. I would have been happy if you were my whole life and my whole reason for being, forever and forever.

"That's the slap in the face, Meg. That you didn't trust my love for you."

His tone and his look were ferocious, but in a way he had just confirmed what she had believed all along. Because his first reaction to her telling him that she couldn't have babies?

He went right to it's for better or worse.

And not the better part.

"We both know for you, not having kids is the worst possible scenario," she said, keeping her composure as best she could. "How could I claim to love someone and set them up for their worst possible scenario?"

"You just won't let it go," he snapped, raking a hand through his hair. "Saint Meg, in charge of the world, in charge of my happiness, whether I like it or not. If I'd known this about you—this supercharged control freak side—I would have never married you in the first place. Because now I'm sorry I did."

He turned and left the room.

The brutality of his words hit her like axe blows, made even more painful because she could see an awful truth in there.

He was right.

In a trance, Meg finished packing her clothes. She walked the path to the still and empty front lobby. The chickens were just starting to crow, promising there was going to be a new day even if she did not want there to be.

She checked her phone. On an impulse, she checked the rideshare app that she used in Ottawa. Imagine that. It had transferred over. Given the earliness of the hour, the sleepiness of Kauai, she was astonished to see a car in the vicinity.

As she clicked on that car, she could not help but think how awful it was that leaving Morgan, again, had a terrible meant-to-be feeling to it.

When he returned to Vancouver, his anger carried Morgan through several weeks. The truth was, he fueled it. He *liked* being angry. It felt powerful. It felt as if his fury kept barriers up where they needed to be.

But in those moments when his guard came down, just before he slept at night, a little girl would come to him.

It wasn't his niece, Kendra.

No, it was a little girl who couldn't accept one good thing for herself, not even a movie with a friend.

Despite his trying to keep the message at bay with anger, Morgan in those sleepless moments at night, the full truth about his wife crept in.

She hadn't run away from him because she couldn't have a baby.

That was just a symptom.

She had run away because she didn't believe she deserved anything for herself. So part of what she had said was true—she could not adjust to the lifestyle. But it wasn't just the wealth and all the things that came with it.

No, what she couldn't adjust to was being

loved. What Meg couldn't adjust to was coming first.

Understanding began to dull the sharp edges
of Morgan's fury. He stood in the dilemma of
the vulnerability that arose to take anger's place.

Did he protect himself?

Or did he summon some remnant of courage
that remained in him, that was willing to risk it
all, one last time, to rescue the woman he loved?

Meg was an absolute mess. She couldn't paint.
She couldn't eat. She couldn't sleep. She was
pretty sure the rent was due and she hadn't paid
it. It was so much worse than the first time she
had left Morgan.

She had seen the look of utter contempt on his
face. She had destroyed the most precious thing
she had ever had.

She had destroyed Morgan's love for her.

There was a loud knocking on the door. From
somewhere in her haze of despair, she thought
it was probably the landlord.

She wanted to ignore it, but what could possibly be made better by an eviction?

"Just a sec," she called. She got out of the rum-
ple of sheets she was tangled in. She knew she
looked like hell. Tangled hair, shadowed eyes,
in her pajamas at three o'clock in the afternoon.

She went out of the bedroom. Her place was

a mess. There were canvasses and easels everywhere. It was the beach series, the paintings she
had not worked on since her return but that she
hadn't been able to part with, either, despite rent
being due and the gallery clamoring for more.

But also displayed on easels, around the living area of the small apartment, were the magical photos from Caylee and Jonathon's wedding.

She had one or two of the bride and groom
displayed, but mostly she had photos of her and
Morgan. His head bent over hers, smiling down
at her, him chasing her playfully through the surf
while she held up her dress. Him kissing her injured shoulder.

The photos were both a torment and a comfort.

But at the moment they added to the cluttered
chaos in her apartment that Meg did not want
the landlord to see.

"Mr. Jones?" she called through the door. "I'm
e-transferring you right now."

No answer.

She opened her banking app, tapped furiously
for a second. "There," she called. "It's done."

"Meg, open the door right now."

Everything in her went still. It wasn't her landlord on the other side of that door. It was Morgan.

And now, because she had spoken, mistaking him for the landlord, she could not pretend she wasn't here.

If she opened that door, he would know how she was suffering. He would see that she wasn't coping without him.

He would see the wedding photos and the beach paintings, her every longing on display for him.

Maybe he would understand how deep the well of her love was, that she was willing to give up her own hope for him to have what he deserved.

What good could come from this?

She closed her eyes. She drew in a deep, shuddering breath. He did not need to know she was suffering.

"Now's not a good time," she called.

"You open this door, or I'm going to break it down."

If she was going to open the door, she needed to run a brush through her hair, maybe try to do something about the shadows under her eyes. She needed not to be in her pajamas looking defeated. She needed to hide the paintings. And especially the wedding photos.

"I'm counting to three."

Suddenly, pretending she was okay felt like way too much effort.

"One."

The back exit out the kitchen window seemed cowardly and pathetic.

"Two."

She was too weak not to open the door for him, too weak to deny herself seeing him again.

"Three."

She opened the door and stood before him, defeated, cowardly, pathetic and weak. The sight of her, and the mess behind her should make him do what everything else had not: turn tail and run. Save himself.

But he didn't turn tail and run.

He looked gorgeous, casual in faded jeans, a white T-shirt, a leather jacket. Some men, dressed like that, would look as if they didn't care about their appearance. Morgan looked ready for a front cover photo shoot for a men's magazine.

He stepped in and took in her place, his eyes resting on each of the photos and paintings, oddly not with surprise, but with a deep *knowing*.

"Caylee asked me to pick the best of the wedding photos for her," she said defensively, when his eyes lingered on the one of him kissing her shoulder.

"There doesn't seem to be that many of Caylee and Jonathon here," he pointed out.

She could feel her face turning crimson, just

as he turned his full attention back and took her in. She realized Morgan looked as though he had been suffering as much as her.

His face was gaunt. There were dark circles under his eyes. He had cut off his beautiful curls, as if he was a soldier going into battle, as if caring for his hair was too much. She felt an absurd desire to touch his shorn head, and maybe she would have but Morgan did not look pathetic or weak.

He looked very, very strong, and his eyes were dark with resolve as they swept over her, missing nothing, taking in all the suffering she could not hide from him.

"Oh, Meggie," he said.

It felt as if she could defend herself against his fury. But that? His fury was, after all, about him. But this empathy was about her.

Morgan was reaching past his anger and caring about her, the one who had caused his anger in the first place.

She could feel some tenderness rising in her that she knew she did not have the strength to hold down. Again, she had to tuck her hands behind her so that she didn't give in to the temptation to touch his hair.

"Come in," she whispered, which was silly, because he was already in. She shut the door behind him.

He strode across her tiny living room, moved

a heap of clothes off the sofa and sat down. As his dark eyes swept over her, it felt as if he knew every single secret about her.

She went over and sank into the chair across from him.

"You shouldn't have come," she said, but the way she drank him in gave lie to those words.

He lifted a broad shoulder. "I needed to come. You needed for me to come."

If she had the energy, she would argue that he had no right to tell her what she needed, but she didn't have the energy.

While she'd been sulking, and not eating, and not sleeping, she really should have been preparing herself for this final battle.

Of course, she had not foreseen it coming, and now she was in no kind of shape to fight all the feelings rising in her.

"I get it now," Morgan told her softly.

"Do you?"

"It was never about not giving me a baby. It was never about not being able to give me back a family."

Her mouth dropped open. "That is not true!"

"Oh, yes it is," he continued with soft determination.

"It was all about that," Meg said fiercely. "It was all about loving you enough to do what needed to be done."

He actually had the nerve to throw back his head and laugh. Then he stopped and took her in with a shake of his head.

"I almost fell for your lies," Morgan told her quietly.

"I've never lied to you."

"Couldn't handle the lifestyle?" he reminded her.

"Okay," she conceded, "that."

"But that lie was okay, wasn't it, because that was for my own good?"

"Correct," she said stiffly.

"It was never about the baby, Meg."

"It was. That's all it was about."

"You know who you're lying to?" he said, his voice so soft, barely a whisper. "Yourself."

She was silent, but she could feel fear pounding inside her chest. Fear, and maybe just a little tiny bit, hope.

"You didn't know what to do with someone putting you first," he said, his voice still soft, caressing, like a touch. "You didn't know how to be the one who got the attention. You didn't know how to be the center of my universe. You didn't know how to accept pampering and gifts and someone genuinely cherishing you. You didn't know how to *accept* love. Only how to give it.

"What you couldn't handle was being with someone who didn't need you to make sacrifices.

What a sense of emptiness that must have caused in you. How could it be love when it wasn't causing you pain, when you weren't scrambling to fix things and giving up every single thing that gave you pleasure?"

Meg's mouth fell open as his arrows of truth hit her heart.

"It must have felt so familiar, so comforting, so satisfying," he continued softly, his eyes never leaving her face, "when you found you couldn't have a baby."

"It was the most devastating moment of my whole life," she said hoarsely.

"No, it wasn't," he challenged her. "It was like coming home. You could give it all up for someone else, the way you've done your entire life. You could be the martyr."

She stared at him. She took in the look in his eyes. There was truth there. And so much love. She began to cry.

"If I let you," he said softly. "You could throw it all away in a misguided sacrifice intended to give me a better life. But, Meg, I'm not letting you. You saved me when I was trying to deal with the loss of my family."

"No," she said through her tears, "you saved me."

"Don't you see? That's what people do. They save each other. You don't overcome those kinds of things alone. That's what we promised when we said *I do*. That we would have each other's backs, that we would heal each other and save each other."

The truth of what Morgan was saying pierced the darkness around Meg like a shard of sunlight finding its way through dark clouds.

She understood, suddenly, the gift she was being given.

Someone who *saw* her completely.

Who saw her flaws and her secrets and was willing to love her anyway. Who had found the bravery to come here, to face, once again, the possibility of her rejection, so that she *knew*.

She was loved exactly as she was.

She did not have to be alone.

That this man would have her back, no matter what.

She could not walk away from what Morgan was offering her. Not this time. She'd been granted a reprieve from the life she had sentenced herself to and she opened to it like a parched flower opening to life-giving rain.

She got up from her chair, crossed the floor to him, lowered herself onto his lap and finally, finally, touched his hair.

She had thought it might feel bristly, like the new growth of whiskers. But it didn't. His short,

short hair felt glorious and soft under her fingertips. She curled her arms around his neck.

She knew it didn't matter to him that she was a mess. In fact, Morgan knew she was a mess, in every possible sense, and he had come anyway.

"Is that yes?" he asked gruffly. "To trying again?"

"Absolutely," she whispered. Her lips found his, and she allowed herself to revel in a sweet sensation she had thought she might never have, ever again.

He kissed her back with tender welcome at first, but the pent-up passion erupted between them.

He held her to him, stood, found his way to the bedroom and put her down on the bed.

"Mrs. Hart," he whispered.

"Mr. Hart," she said, and it felt like a vow. She opened her arms to him, and he came into them.

They were home.

A long time later, nestled in each other's arms, she reveled in the simple rise and fall of his naked chest under her cheek.

"I think we should go to Hawaii and renew our vows," he said sleepily.

"Isn't that what we just did?"

He stroked her hair. "I want to do it again. We'll do it the right way this time."

"It was right last time," she said.

"I want to celebrate it with the world, the way Jonathon and Caylee did."

She could tell it meant the world to him, and she did love the idea of including all their friends in this: the hope and the healing of love.

"Is your shoulder completely better?"

Meg giggled. "You couldn't tell?"

"Okay, because I'm not going back to Kauai until you can snorkel."

"I could be ready for tomorrow," she said huskily.

"No! I'm sure it will take some time to make all the arrangements."

"It won't really. We have wedding-in-a-box. We could probably have all those clothes that Caylee ended up not using."

"I loved you in that dress," he agreed. "Still, accommodations, invitations—"

"Should we say we'll return to Kauai to renew our vows with all our friends as soon as it's humanly possible?"

"Finally," Morgan said tenderly, "we're on the same page."

"Forever," she agreed softly.

EPILOGUE

Three years later

IT WAS AN absolutely perfect summer day. A sun-on-pine-scented breeze drifted through Morgan's open office window, and he looked out at Okanagan Lake. The surface of its navy blue water was sprinkled with thousands of glinting sunshine stars.

He was getting some last-minute paperwork done before company started arriving at Sarah's Reach for the weekend.

He heard the shriek of a child, followed by a splash, gales of laughter and then Meg's quiet voice in the background.

Morgan got up from his desk and took the adjoining door out onto the deeply shaded deck that wrapped around the whole cottage.

It was a better vantage point to see them.

His family.

They were out there on the float, the four children, the boys shoving at each other, while Ophelia ran joyous circles around them, squealing. Meg sat cross-legged at the center of it all with Marie, thumb in mouth, fighting a losing battle to keep her eyes open. Meg looked, in the middle of that happy summer chaos, calm and light-filled.

Meg's beach series—those whimsical paintings of families enjoying the sand and water on perfect summer days—had become her bestselling work ever.

Looking at this scene before him, Morgan couldn't help but wonder: How had she been able to paint the future? Had it been a premonition? Or had she literally been *drawing* this scene, playing out before him now, into reality?

Of course, as was the way with the world, this was not the life he and Meg had planned. Not even close.

They had investigated every option that would bring them a baby. They had looked at everything from in vitro to surrogacy. They had been approved by a global adoption agency. Unlike many in their position, Morgan and Meg Hart had unlimited resources.

Ironically, it was not their resources, in the end, that brought them to family. It was that worst of human travesties.

War.

A friend had told them, almost in passing,

about a story she had heard. A bombed building collapsing, a mother and father killed, three children and a baby pulled, unharmed, protected by the bodies of their parents, from the rubble.

Though, of course, unharmed was a relative term.

He often thought—especially now—of those protestors he and Meg had seen in Hawaii, waving their signs and chanting their slogans against war, oblivious to the fact that their anger was the very thing war sprang from.

And then there had been Kamelei, keeping the values of her culture safe in the face of an ironic assault against it by people who claimed to be against the importation of values from other cultures.

His and Meg's relationship with the shop owner had deepened over the years. Meg had done some artwork for her that had ended up being printed onto fabric for her clothing line.

Morgan hoped he carried some of the things Kamelei continued to teach them about *aloha* within him.

Problems could not be solved from the same place they had sprung.

Love was the only force that changed things.

And love in action took on a force and power like nothing else that existed.

Life had taught Morgan the hardest of lessons.

All his wealth and all his power and all his success had not been able to hold back calamity.

He was a man painfully aware he could not save the world.

And yet, that didn't mean he couldn't try. That didn't mean he couldn't save some.

Morgan was not sure his resources had ever been put to a better use than finding those children. He had been pushed by a force so compelling he could, to this day, not explain it.

He and Megan had known what they would do even before they met those children. Max, eight, Stefan, six, Ophelia, three, and Marie, at that time just turned a year.

Those children. Max, radiating anger and lashing out. Stefan, hostile to the world, cold and withdrawn. Ophelia, completely shut down, a zombie child. And Marie, a baby who could not sleep more than fifteen minutes without waking up screaming and terrified.

He and Meg had known, without a single word passing between them, that they had not, after all, been broken by their losses. Their losses had prepared them. For this.

They were possibly the two people most qualified to love children that some might say—and did say—were damaged beyond repair by the horrific harms they had survived.

But in that moment, meeting those children

for the first time, this is what Morgan and Meg knew. They had been made for this challenge.

They had also felt loss so crushing it felt as if you could not breathe, let alone rise from it.

But both of them also knew this: beneath all that blackness, beneath the char of a life destroyed, a spark of spirit remained, a spark that could not, ever, be extinguished.

It was a tiny ember that love slowly fanned back to life.

Love took so many different forms, and he had seen this firsthand when he had watched Meg thrown into the arena of parenting four damaged children. It was the job she'd been born to do, her calling.

And in those first days and months, her love might not have looked like love at all. By instinct, she had been strict, firm, disciplined, unflagging.

"We are raising people to be responsible," she told him, after she'd put Max in his room for beheading a teddy bear. "We can't get there if we teach them it's okay to be mean, self-pitying, entitled, pampered.

"We can't get there if we give them the message *Oh, poor you, look what the world has done. Let's make up for it every day for the rest of our lives forever.*"

Having had a brother with a disability, Meg

was uniquely placed. She knew it was too easy to let sympathy dissolve boundaries, to let pity accept the unacceptable.

"People," she told him, "do not have a ticket to be obnoxious because they've been victims."

As it turned out, what those children needed most, particularly at first, was not hugs and cuddles. What they needed was structure. Bedtime. Bath time. Storytime. Chores. A meal on the table every single day at the very same time.

They needed a sense that they were part of something bigger, necessary to something bigger.

That was how love had come to them.

And made them a family.

Love whispered of all their tragedies. *It's true. You will never be the same.*

But you will find reason in your suffering.

You will be led to your purpose.

You will be more than you were before: more compassionate, more intuitive, more humble, more able to surrender to a life path you have realized you cannot always control.

This, really, was what it was to be human. It was to suffer, and to rise from the suffering, not healed, but changed, altered in fundamental ways.

It was exactly the promise Morgan had seen in Meg's painting all those years ago. On the wings of love, you will rise out of the ashes.

His and Meg's life experiences had made them the perfect parents to these grieving children.

Sarah's Reach had also risen from the ashes. The cabin rebuilt, but just like Meg and Morgan, she would be more than she was before.

Sometimes, late at night, Morgan, who had always considered himself the most pragmatic of men, thought he heard the giggles of Kendra and James in the hallways of the new house, sometimes he thought he heard the rumble of his brother's laugh. Sometimes, he thought he heard a wheelchair on the wooden floors, and caught a shadowy glimpse of a boy he had never met. Sometimes, he felt as if his sister-in-law looked at Max and Stefan, at Ophelia and Marie, and touched his shoulder.

Whispered an approving, grateful *yes*.

Whether they were really there or whether they were a figment of his imagination, Morgan knew he and Meg were using their lives to honor the love that they grew out of.

On the other side of the bluff, he could hear hammers hitting wood, the voices of men calling to each other.

It was the first phase. Someday, a camp would be here, in this place where his family had known so much joy.

Hart's Reach would gather the children of

trauma, and give them a respite from whatever horrors the world had brought them.

It would give them a small window of hope. It would show them there were safe places in the world. It would show them there would be laughter again.

It would just be that little breath of love that would fan to life that flicker of hope that lived, unquenchable, in each human heart.

As he watched, Stefan, who had been pushed off the float, hoisted himself back on it. He chased his bigger brother, and they wrestled playfully until Max pretended he had been over-whelmed, and they both fell in the water.

Right now, it felt as if every single thing they had been through had led to this moment. From the other direction, Morgan heard a car door slam, and Caylee's voice, calling to her and Jon-athon's twins.

"Joseph, Jolie, do not go that way, do not—"

Morgan could imagine Jonathon chasing after those rambunctious children, tucking one under each arm.

Caylee's voice came again, "It's like herding cats…"

In the last three years, almost every single member of that wedding party had gotten mar-ried.

Part of it, Morgan knew, was because they

were just at that stage of life where people began to settle.

But he also wondered how much of those beautiful, blissful times they had all spent together on the island of Kauai had influenced this.

He and Meg had renewed their vows there six months after their reconciliation. The same group of people had come back.

Meg laughingly called it wedding-in-a-box since they had used all those items of clothing that had been the backup plan for Caylee.

So, her dress did not equal the budget of a small country for a year, and yet as Meg had walked across the sand toward him, Morgan had been aware that there had never been a more beautiful bride than her.

The sound of a door opening jarred him out of that memory.

"Hello?" Jonathon called.

And then he heard little feet running, and Jolie calling out, "Unkie? Unkie? Unkie?"

A shiver went up and down his spine, because it was so like moments he'd had with his niece, Kendra.

He and Meg had lost family, and that grief was always there. And yet, so was an understanding that family was bigger than blood bonds, and that everything you lost would come back to you, maybe in a different form, but it would come back to you nonetheless.

Came back to you, multiplied.

Look at those children out on the dock right now.

Their friends who had married were all starting to have children. Again, it was that time of life, though Meg liked to claim it was because she had touched the Hawaiian fertility god, Lono. She said that what you wished for yourself blessed your friends, as well.

Sarah's Reach was filling up with families again. Laughter. Skinned knees and kisses, the smell of marshmallows, the shriek of warm bodies hitting cold water.

This is what he and Meg had said when they got married.

And then Jonathon and Caylee.

And then their other friends.

This is what they said when they had babies and sheltered children in need, and created families in an uncertain and an unpredictable world where there were no guarantees.

These were acts of pure hope.

These were the arrows manifested by faith. They carried a belief in the goodness of life, and the truth of love. Tentatively, they were removed from the quiver, set against a taut string, that bow stretched back and back and back.

And when it could be pulled no farther, when the arm that held it was trembling with effort, then the arrow was released.

Shooting forward in a beautiful, powerful arc.

Soaring, unstoppable, toward its destination. This was pure faith in the power of love, to send this arrow to a place only partially visible to the archer, to a place he would never be able to explore completely.

Love sent its arrows, strong and true, toward the greatest of all mysteries.

The future.

* * * * *

If you enjoyed this story,
check out these other great reads
from Cara Colter

The Billionaire's Festive Reunion
Accidentally Engaged to the Billionaire
Winning Over the Brooding Billionaire
Hawaiian Nights with the Best Man

All available now!

Harlequin® Reader Service

Enjoyed your book?

Try the perfect subscription for Romance readers and get more great books like this delivered right to your door.

See why over 10+ million readers have tried Harlequin Reader Service.

Start with a Free Welcome Collection with free books and a gift—valued over $20.

Choose any series in print or ebook. See website for details and order today:

TryReaderService.com/subscriptions

RSBPA2409